Enid Blyton's
HAPPY ADVENTURE TALES

Enid Blyton's

HAPPY ADVENTURE TALES

PURNELL

London

SBN 361 01810 x

Published in 1971 by Purnell, London
Text © 1971 by Darrell Waters Ltd.
Artwork © 1971 by B.P.C. Publishing Ltd.
All rights reserved
Made and printed in Great Britain by Purnell & Sons Ltd.
Paulton (Somerset) and London.

CONTENTS

Colin is a Good Policeman

COLIN was saving up to buy a pair of skates. He had put all his Christmas money into his money-box and had put his Saturday pennies there too, and a sixpence that his Daddy had given him for sweeping the snow away from the front path.

The money-box was a fat pig with a slit in its back. The money came out of its tummy, for there was a lock there, and when Colin put in the key and undid the lock, a little trap-door opened and the money fell out.

"Next week I shall be able to buy myself a pair of skates!" said Colin one morning, as he counted out his money. "Hurrah! Then I'll be able to go skating with Ned and Bill! I *shall* feel grand!"

But something horrid happened before he bought his skates. A burglar came one night, broke into Colin's house, and took Colin's money-box, Mummy's purse, Daddy's lovely field-glasses, some silver from the sideboard, and a beautiful cup that Daddy had won for a golf prize.

Mummy was dreadfully upset. The policeman came and took notes about everything. Daddy told him to be sure and catch the thief if he could, for Mummy had had a lot of money in her purse.

"And I had a lot in my money-box pig," said Colin, almost crying. "I saved it up to buy some skates. Now my money is all gone. Please do catch the thief, policeman."

"I'll do my best," said the policeman, shutting his note-book. "Let me see where he got in, please."

The burglar had got in at a small window that led into the larder. The policeman made some more notes, and then went.

The thief was not caught, because the policeman had no idea who the burglar could be. Day after day went by and still there was no news. Colin got more and more impatient.

"Mummy," he said, "won't that thief ever be caught? What about my money-pig? I wanted to buy my skates with the money this week. Can't I get it back?"

"No, dear, not unless the burglar is caught," said Mummy. "And it doesn't seem to me as if he will be, now."

"But, Mummy, he simply *must* be caught, because I want the money for my skates," said Colin in despair.

"Well, dear, unless you catch him yourself, I don't see how you're going to get back your pig," said Mummy, laughing. "The policeman has done his best."

Colin went out into the garden, nearly crying. To think he had lost all his money like that, when he had saved up so hard. It was too bad.

Then he thought again of what Mummy had said—

"Unless you catch him yourself, I don't see how you're going to get back your pig."

"If only I *could* find out who it was," thought Colin. "But I don't know how to begin. I don't know if the burglar was tall or short, fat or thin. I don't know anything about him at all." He thought hard for a minute, and then he frowned. "Wait a minute—I *do* know something about him! He must have been very small to get through that tiny window!"

13

He jumped up and went to the larder window. Certainly it was very tiny. Colin jumped up to the sill —and he noticed that as he jumped he left deep marks in the bed below. And there, beside his own marks, were two other marks, made by someone else!

He jumped down to look at them. They must have been made by the burglar, for the ground was soft, and there had been no rain to wash out any marks since the robbery. They were deep, too, just as if the man had jumped up to the sill as Colin had done.

The little boy suddenly felt excited. He knew two things about the burglar now—he was small, because the window was very tiny, and he had big feet, because the marks outside in the bed were large. Good!

Colin found his mother's measuring tape and measured the footmarks carefully. Then he measured his father's slippers, and found that the footmarks were even bigger than the slippers. The burglar had bigger feet than Daddy's!

"A small man with very big feet," said Colin to himself. "What else?"

He sat and thought—and then he rubbed his hands together, for he had thought of something else. Mummy had said how queer it was that Micky the dog hadn't barked at the burglar that night, for Micky always barked at strangers.

"Well, if Micky didn't bark, he must have known the man's voice and smell," said Colin to himself. "And if he knew the man, it means that the robber must have come here often and spoken to Micky and given him tit-bits to make friends with him. I'm getting on! I'm looking for a small man with big feet, someone who comes here fairly often, and whom Micky is friendly with."

Colin felt tremendously excited. He went to the window and jumped up to the sill again. He thought he would jump down into the larder and see how much noise he made. So down into the larder he jumped—and as he did so his coat caught on a nail just below the window and tore.

15

"Bother!" said Colin, and looked angrily at the nail. And caught on that nail was a piece of brown cloth with a little red line running through it!

"Gracious!" said Colin. "That's not a bit of *my* coat! The burglar must have caught his coat on that nail just as I did—and this is a bit of the coat that he wore then! Oh, I *am* getting on! Yes, I really am. I know the robber was a small man with big feet, who comes here often, is friendly with Micky, and wears a brown coat that has a little red pattern running through it!"

The little boy rushed into the garden and thought of all the men who came to the house. Not the milkman—he was tall. Not the butcher—he had small feet. Not the dustman, nor the postman, nor the baker, because Micky wouldn't be friendly with any of them, and barked madly as soon as they appeared.

"What about the window-cleaner?" thought Colin. "No—he only comes once a month and, besides, he is fat. He could never get into that tiny window."

There was the man who brought the eggs—but Micky hated him. There was the paper-man—it might be him. He was very friendly with Micky, and he was small too. Also he wore a brown coat!

"I don't remember if he has big feet, though," thought Colin, jumping up, excited. "I must go and see."

The paper-man lived down the road. Colin did hope it wasn't him, because he was a nice man, and always ready for a joke. He was standing at the door of his shop as Colin ran up.

Yes, his coat was brown, but it had a blue pattern running through it instead of red—and his feet were not even as large as Colin's Daddy's feet; so it couldn't be the paper-man. Colin was glad.

And then suddenly the little boy thought of the man who sometimes came to dig in the garden. He was a bad-tempered little fellow, and Mummy didn't like him. But Daddy said he needed help, and so he gave him a job in the garden whenever he could, and Mummy made him up parcels of bread and cake and fruit.

"We must always help others who are not so well off as we are," Mummy said to Colin, so the little boy had given Walters, the odd-job man, a whole shilling out of his own money at Christmas-time. He had emptied his money-pig and chosen the shilling himself to give to Walters.

"Could it be Walters?" wondered Colin. "He is quite small enough to creep in at the window—and I know he has big feet because I heard him grumbling that he couldn't wear Daddy's boots, they were too small. Micky likes him because he throws him bits of his bread. But I simply *can't* remember the coat he wears."

Now the very next day the odd-job man came again to dig the garden over. But as it was too frosty Daddy said he could chop wood instead. Colin went down the garden to tell him, and to the little boy's great excitement he saw that Walters was wearing a brown coat with a little red pattern in it—and at one side it was torn!

Colin's heart beat fast. So it *was* Walters who had been mean enough to steal from Daddy and Mummy, who had always been so kind to him!

The boy ran into the house as fast as he could and shouted for his Daddy. "Daddy! I want you! I know who the burglar was last week! Oh, do get my money-pig from him and Mummy's purse and your golf-cup!"

"Colin! Whatever do you mean?" said Daddy, astonished.

"Listen, Daddy," said Colin. "I know all about the burglar. He's small, because he couldn't get in at the larder window if he were big. He has large feet, bigger than yours, because I measured his footmarks in the bed below the window. He's a friend of Micky's, because Micky didn't bark at him—and that means he comes here fairly often—and he wears a brown coat made of cloth like this!"

He gave his Daddy the bit of torn cloth. "I found it caught on the nail just below the larder window," he said. "And, Daddy, the burglar is Walters! He has got a coat on like that this morning, and it's torn!"

Daddy listened, getting more and more astonished. Mummy couldn't believe her ears.

"Why, you're a splendid policeman, Colin," she said.

"Oh, Daddy—I never did like Walters. You were always so kind to him, and now see how he has returned your kindness! What are you going to do?"

"Ring up the police!" said Daddy, and he did. Well, Colin was quite right, for when the policeman went round to Walters' house, the first thing he saw on the mantelpiece was Colin's money-pig! And in a drawer were Mummy's purse, quite empty, and Daddy's field-glasses. The golf-cup was in a cupboard, but the side-board silver was gone. Walters had sold it.

Colin was so pleased to get back his pig—but, alas, it was empty! The thief had taken all the money out. Colin nearly wept with disappointment. "I shan't get my skates after all!" he said.

But he did. The policemen were delighted to have found the robber, for Walters had not only robbed Colin's Daddy and Mummy, but many others besides. And soon, no doubt, he would have taken things from other houses too. The police were glad to have found the thief, for they had been looking for him for a long time—and what do you think they did? They sent to the toy-shop, and they bought a fine pair of skates for Colin!

The little boy opened the parcel, and saw the note with it: "A pair of skates for a good policeman!" and he squealed in delight.

"They are much finer than the ones I had saved up to buy. Oh, I *am* lucky!"

And you should just see him whizzing along on them! Goodness me, he goes as fast as the wind!

The Prisoner in the Cave

"LET'S go and play in the wood on Windy Hill," said Michael. "It's a lovely sunny day, and there won't be many more chances this autumn of going there."

"All right," said Janet. "I'd like that. We might see if any squirrels are about. We may see them collecting nuts and acorns."

So off they went. The woods were lovely. The children wandered through the trees, and then saw a red squirrel. A *red* one! How lovely. They had only seen grey ones before.

"Quick! Let's follow it," said Michael, so they tracked it through the woods. It bounded lightly along the boughs of the trees, then down to the ground to pick up an acorn.

"We might see where it has its hidey-hole," said Janet softly. "Isn't it lovely! I do like the way it sits up, don't you?"

"Oh—it's gone," said Michael. "It rushed up that tree and into the next, and it's gone. We must have frightened it."

Janet looked round and about. "Where exactly are we?" she said. "I've never been on this part of the hill before. Oh, Michael, do you think we're near the hill-caves. We have never been able to find them, you know."

"We'll look round a bit and see," said Michael. "I know they're somewhere half-way up the hill, and that's about where we are."

They wandered round a bit, and then Janet called out in excitement: "Look! There's a cave, surely? That dark patch over there."

They ran to where Janet was pointing. Yes, it *was* a cave! How exciting!

"Shall we go in?" said Janet. "It looks a bit dark and gloomy."

"Of course we'll go in," said Michael. "We must explore! Caves are fun—you never know what you'll find in them or where they lead to, or where they end. Think of all the thousands and thousands of caves under the earth that nobody has ever been in—how I'd like to explore them all!"

They peeped in at the cave entrance. It was certainly dark in the cave. "Have you got a torch?" asked Janet. "I'm not going in unless you have."

"Yes, I've got one," said Michael. "It's the one I had for my birthday last week. Come on."

He switched on his torch and the beam lighted up the cave at once. It was narrow and rather long. It smelt a bit damp and musty, and Janet didn't like it very much.

"Let's play we've been shipwrecked and found a cave to shelter in," said Michael. "We'll make it our home. Go and get some dry bracken and we'll make a bed. There's a kind of shelf here at the side of the cave that will do beautifully for one."

Janet went to get some bracken. Soon the two children had made a very fine bed to lie on. "Now we really ought to make a fire at the cave entrance to keep away wild animals," said Michael.

But they couldn't do that because neither of them had any matches. So they put a little pile of sticks at the entrance, pretending that it really was alight.

"I've found a tiny stream running down the hill just nearby," said Janet, coming back with some more bracken. "That's lucky for us. We shall have water to drink whilst we're shipwrecked."

"What about food?" asked Michael. "I suppose we could eat nuts and things, like the squirrels. There might be a few blackberries, too."

They managed to find a few late blackberries, rather squashy and small, and they picked up some acorns.

"Not much food for two poor shipwrecked sailors!" said Janet solemnly, as she put them down on a tiny ledge above their "bed".

"Now let's play being shipwrecked right from the beginning," said Michael. "We stagger up the hill, moaning—we find the cave and stumble into it gladly—we fall on our bed and sleep for hours. Let's do that."

So, much to the surprise of two rabbits who were watching from under a bush, the two children came staggering up the hillside, giving strange moans. Janet even stopped to pretend to wring water out of her clothes. "Wet and cold!" she kept saying. "Shipwrecked and almost drowned."

"Nobody saved but us," said Michael, wringing water out of his jersey.

"Look—there's a cave!" said Janet, so suddenly that she made Michael jump. "We must rest. I can go no farther."

"It may be a cave for wild animals," said Michael. "Perhaps they sleep there at night."

"Then we will build a fire to keep them away," said Janet, who was really very good at pretending.

They stumbled into the cave and flung themselves down on the bed of bracken at the side. Janet gave some realistic groans. Then she fell back, pretending to be asleep. Michael did the same. For a minute or two there was complete silence in the cave.

And then something very surprising happened. Footsteps came up to the cave and somebody peeped in. The children heard the steps and sat up.

"Hist!" said Michael in Janet's ear. "Savages! Don't move!"

At the cave entrance stood a man. He was bareheaded, but they could not see his face. He carried something in his hands. It looked like a bag of some sort—a paper bag.

He came right into the cave, switching on a torch as he did so. He did not swing the beam of light to the side of the cave, but straight in front of him. So he didn't catch sight of the silent children sitting up on their bed of bracken. To their intense surprise he walked right to the back of the cave—and then disappeared!

They heard faint sounds in the distance. Where had the man gone? Was there another cave right at the back—or a passage or something?

Michael clutched Janet and whispered again. "What's he doing back there? Does he live here, do you suppose?"

"Oh dear—if he's a tramp who lives in these caves he won't be very pleased at finding us here," said Janet. "Let's go."

But before they could go they heard sounds again, and the man came back. He carried something else in his hands now. Michael strained his eyes to see what it was. It was a big jug!

"A jug!" he thought. "He must be going to get some water. So he does live here! I bet he's going to that little stream."

The man went out of the cave. The children did not like to escape just then in case the man saw them, because the stream was only just nearby. So they covered themselves with the bracken and lay quite still, waiting for him to come back. Janet's heart was beating rather fast. It all seemed rather queer somehow.

The man came back almost at once, carrying the jug carefully as if it were full of water. He disappeared at the back of the cave again.

"He *must* live there," said Michael. "He's taken food and drink to some cave at the back that he has made into his home."

"Well, let's go, then," said Janet. "It's getting dark."

But before they could go the man came back again, without the jug, and walked straight out of the cave and down the hill.

"Why—he's gone," said Michael, puzzled. "Where's he gone? Why doesn't he stay in his cave now it's getting dark?"

"Michael—listen—what's that noise?" suddenly said Janet, clutching at Michael's arm. They both listened. A curious, faraway noise came from the back of the cave. What was it? A moan—a groan—a howl? And who was making it, back there in the heart of the hill?

"Oh, Michael—there's a prisoner in the cave behind

28

this one," said Janet, frightened. "There is, there is! And it's he who is making that awful noise."

"It does seem queer," said Michael, not liking it at all. "It really looks as if there must be somebody who is being kept prisoner—the man certainly took food and drink there."

"Probably he comes every day to bring some," said Janet. "Goodness—it's all very strange. What shall we do?"

"Do you think we'd better see if we can find the prisoner?" asked Michael, who wasn't really feeling very brave at the moment.

"Oh, I'd be scared to," said Janet. "But I suppose we *ought* to try and rescue him. Shall we—shall we just go to the back of the cave and see where it leads?"

"All right," said Michael, switching on his torch. "But we'd better hurry, because it will be dark soon!"

They went on tiptoe to the back of the cave. At first they could see nothing but rocky wall—then Michael's torch picked out a small opening.

"Look—that's where the man went through. I bet there's a passage there, leading to somewhere else."

A strange sound came booming up from behind the cave they were in. That was enough for the two children. They turned and fled, trampling down the twigs they had arranged for their fire. They didn't stop running till they were half-way down the hill!

"Oh dear—what dreadful cowards we are," said Janet, panting, "to leave that poor prisoner behind, moaning like that. Well, it's so dark I simply daren't go back. We'd better go home and talk about it."

So they went down the hill and soon came to the town they lived in. As they passed the bus-stop a bus came up and a man got on to it. Janet pulled at Michael's arm.

"Look—isn't that the bare-headed man we saw in our cave? Yes—it is. He's catching the bus, so he *doesn't* live in the cave. There *is* a prisoner there that he takes food and water to!"

30

The children went home. They would tell their mother. She would know what to do. But she was out. What a pity! "Well, let's pop in next door and tell Harry and Mark," said Michael. "They'll be thrilled."

They were! In fact they were so thrilled that they wanted to solve the mystery themselves and not tell any grown-up.

"Don't tell your mother," begged Harry. "Let's all go up there tomorrow afternoon and find out where the prisoner is and what his name is, and why he's being kept in the cave. This is all very exciting, you know. How lucky you were to go to those caves this afternoon!"

So it was decided that the secret should be kept, and the next day all four should go up to the hill-cave and explore thoroughly what lay behind it. They would rescue the prisoner by themselves!

"I don't believe tomorrow will *ever* come!" said Janet that night. But it did, of course—and brought a very exciting day with it!

The next afternoon Michael, Janet, Harry and Mark met outside in the road. Each of them had a torch with a new battery in it. Nobody was going to risk being in the dark!

"Isn't this exciting!" said Janet, who felt very brave now that she and Michael had two big boys with them. "What shall we find, I wonder? Shall we see that man again—the one who took in food and water?

"Not if he comes at the same time as he did yesterday," said Michael, looking at his watch. "We're too early to see him if he comes at the same time. As we think we saw him going off by bus yesterday evening it's likely he *comes* here by bus, too —and probably catches the same one each time."

"We'll be able to explore without being afraid he'll pounce on us, then," said Janet thankfully. "This way, Harry—up between these trees—and then to the left. Yesterday was the first time we'd been this way."

Soon they came to the cave opening. They stood and looked at it. The entrance was dark and quiet. Not a sound was to be heard except for the wind in the trees. "There it is," said Michael. "The Cave of Mystery."

"Rather thrilling," said Harry. "Jolly good place to keep a prisoner in. Nobody ever comes here, I should think. I suppose they've tied the prisoner up. Poor fellow! It must be awful to be kept here day after day in a dark cave. Do you suppose it's somebody who has been kidnapped and held to ransom?"

"Gracious!" said Janet. "Do things like that *really* happen nowadays?"

"Of course," said Mark. "Now come on—we'll go in very quietly, just in *case* there's a keeper there— that man you saw yesterday, or somebody else. They might perhaps have someone keeping guard on the prisoner."

Things began to seem even more thrilling. The four children went quietly into the cave, the beams of their torches flashing brightly.

"There's the bed of bracken we made," said Michael, shining his torch on to the tumbled pile of bracken. "We were lying there, pretending to be shipwrecked sailors asleep when the man came in."

But Harry and Mark weren't interested in the bracken. They wanted to see what was at the back of the cave. Soon they were shining their torches there, and saw the small, dark opening in the rocky wall.

"Yes—this leads to somewhere," said Harry. "Come on—let's squeeze through. I say—this is exciting, isn't it!"

Harry went through the rather narrow opening first. Janet went next, then Michael, then Mark. They found themselves in a dark passage smelling very damp. Its walls were wet with moisture, and in some places the roof was so low that their heads brushed against it.

The passage wound along for some way. At one place they had to climb over a mound of earth. Harry flashed his torch up to the roof and pointed there. "See," he whispered, "there's been a roof-fall just here. Let's hope one doesn't come whilst we're in the passage. It would be awful if we were cut off by a fall of earth."

This was a dreadful thought, and Janet didn't like it at all. She half thought she would turn back and wait for the boys when they returned. But no—she couldn't possibly do that. They would say scornfully that that was just like a girl! So Janet went on with the boys.

And then they heard the mournful sounds again! They came echoing up the passage, half howl, half moan, and died away into what sounded like miserable whimpers. The children stood as if they were frozen. The prisoner must indeed be unhappy if he cried out like that!

"Shall we go on?" whispered Michael. "Or—or shall we turn back?"

Nobody particularly wanted to go on at that moment, but on the other hand nobody wanted to leave the mystery unsolved! They must go on—it was the only thing to do.

So on they went, and almost at once came out into a vast cave with a sandy floor. It seemed much drier than the outside cave and the passage. The roof rose high, and in places the children's torches could not pick it up. They stood in awe, looking round. There seemed something very grand and mysterious about such a large cave. Perhaps it had been used by animals scores of thousands of years back—and then by men and their families sheltering here safely from storm and cold and fierce animals.

"We should find plenty of bones and things here if we had time to look," whispered Harry. And then he jumped because his whisper was taken up by the echoes in the cave and a great whispering sounded all round them, fading away at last.

"Gracious!" said Janet, startled into speech.

"Shus, shus, shus," said the echoes at once. They were repeating the last part of "Gracious".

And then the noises started again, but this time the howls and groans were taken by the echoes and magnified so tremendously that the whole cave seemed to be full of prisoners moaning, whimpering and howling. The four children clutched one another, holding their breath.

"Goodness—where did that noise come from?" said Mark, the echoes fastening on his words as he spoke them.

"From over there," said Harry. "Come on. I think I can see something." They went over to where his torch shone its straight beam. The children saw that a big stone was rolled in front of the entrance to another cave—a small cave evidently, for the top of the opening was only as high as their waists,

"That's where the prisoner is," said Mark, excited. "Look—here's some water spilt just outside. The man must have spilt that when he brought the jug here yesterday."

"Shall we call to the prisoner?" said Janet.

"Yes," said Harry. "Hey there! Are you a prisoner? Who are you?"

There was no answer at all—yet the four children felt certain that the prisoner was listening intently. In fact, they could all hear his quick breathing as they listened for an answer. And then Janet suddenly felt sure she could hear *two* people breathing. Yes—she could!

"I believe there are *two* prisoners in there," she said. "Why don't they answer us?"

Mark called loudly. "We're friends. You don't need to be afraid. We're just going to roll away this stone and then you'll be free."

Still no answer. How very queer! Surely the prisoners could just call out, "Set us free," or something like that!

But they didn't. Except for their quick breathing, which almost seemed to be a panting, there was no sound from them at all.

The children began to have doubts about moving away the stone. What kind of prisoners were these? They really must be mad not to answer friends who were willing to rescue them. Then Mark made up his mind.

"We'll move the stone a little way," he said, "and shine our torches in. Then we shall see what prisoners are there. We can roll the stone back quickly if we don't like the look of them."

"I wonder why *they* don't try and move the stone themselves," said Michael suddenly. "It seems jolly queer."

"Their hands are bound, I expect," said Mark. "Now come on, Harry. Help me to shift this stone a bit." Harry helped him, and the stone moved a little from the entrance.

Then Mark shone his torch in at the crack. He gave a sudden exclamation, and Janet screamed! Four eyes gleamed at them from the darkness at the back of a small cave—fierce eyes, angry eyes! Janet wanted to run away.

"Why—they're animals," said Harry in the greatest surprise. "Not men at all. Here, shine your torch in, Michael; and you, too, Janet. We'll make a better light then to see what the prisoners really are."

At the back of the little cave stood two beautiful dogs, greyhounds, with big, mournful eyes and long noses. They were too frightened to move as the light of the four torches shone into their eyes.

"Look at that—dogs! *Greyhounds!*" said Mark, amazed. "No wonder they didn't shout out to us when we shouted to them. No wonder, too, that we couldn't make out what that mournful moaning, howling noise was—it was the poor things howling in misery and loneliness!"

"Oh, poor, poor dogs!" said Janet, almost crying. "Get them out, Mark. Pull away the stone. Let them free."

The three boys tugged at the stone and it came away from the cave entrance. But still the dogs wouldn't come out. It was clear that they were cowed and terrified. Janet, suddenly brave because she was so full of pity, crawled in to them. She saw the jug of water upset on the floor, and a dish empty of food. The dogs cowered away from her.

She stroked and petted them. One licked her face timidly, and then they both made up their minds that this was no enemy but a friend. They fell on the little girl with whimpers of delight and licked her till she was wet all over!

"Stolen greyhounds!" said Harry grimly. "Champions, I expect. Kept here till the hue and cry after them died down, and then they would be shipped across to Ireland or somewhere and sold for large sums."

"Let's take the poor things home with us," begged Janet. "We can't just leave them here I'm sure they must want a drink—their jug of water is upset."

The two dogs pressed closely against the little girl as the four children went across the vast cave to the little passage. They were soon out in the first cave and then made their way thankfully into the open air. The dogs soon found their high spirits and gambolled about.

How surprised the children's parents were to see them arriving with two beautiful greyhounds, and to hear their strange story. The police were told at once, and two men were sent up to the cave to watch for the man who brought the food and water.

"They'll catch him all right," said the inspector, fondling the lovely dogs. "There's been a lot of this dog-stealing lately. I shall soon be able to find out who are the owners of these beauties!"

"Can we keep them if you don't find out?" asked Janet eagerly. But, of course, the owners were found that very evening, and the children had to say goodbye to the two prisoners they had rescued.

That wasn't quite the end of the story, though. One day a small box arrived, with air-holes in it—and what do you suppose the children found in the box when they opened it? Yes—a tiny greyhound puppy, the dearest little thing you ever saw! It was for Janet and Michael, because they had really been the ones to discover the prisoners.

"But, of course, we'll share him with you, Mark and Harry," said Janet. "He shall belong to all four of us."

So he does—and I wish he belonged to me, too!

Little Lucky Man

ONCE Margery had a tiny little man out of a Christmas cracker. He was so small that he wasn't much taller than a pin!

"Oh, *look*!" cried Margery in delight, as he fell out on to the table. "A teeny little man—dressed in blue and white—with the tiniest smile on his face!" She held him up. "Look, Mummy, isn't he sweet? I know he's a lucky man!"

Well, it did really seem as if the little man was lucky, because all kinds of things began to happen to Margery after that. She had invitations to four parties and a pantomime. She found a shilling she had lost. She was given a big box of chocolates by an uncle who had never given her anything before.

"I'm sure it's this tiny man who's bringing me luck!" said Margery to Jack, her brother. "Ever since I've had him nice things have been happening to me. Oh, little lucky man, I shall keep you safe. I should hate to lose you. You might take your good luck away with you!"

"Lend him to me," said Jack, who had not had very good luck that week. Daddy had spanked him for being cheeky. He had lost a sixpence Mummy had given him for shopping, and he had broken a jug.

"No. You're so careless," said Margery, holding the little lucky man tightly. "You'd lose him! You always lose everything, Jack. You even lost your new ball the day after you had it."

"You're really mean," said Jack. "You won't even spare me a day's good luck! Well, one day I'll get your

43

little lucky man, and I'll hide him where you can't find him and take him about with me. Then, maybe, all kinds of nice things will happen to me, too!"

"You're not to take him away from me!" cried Margery. "You'll only lose him. I shall be so upset then."

Well, Margery simply would *not* lend Jack her lucky man, and, really, it wasn't very surprising, because Jack was certainly a very careless boy. He was always breaking his toys, and had lost his two new handkerchiefs, as well as his ball. But Jack felt certain that if only Margery would lend him the lucky man even for a day he might find everything he had lost, and get some more good luck besides.

He grumbled about it to his Mother. "I do think Margery might lend me the lucky man. Then things would go right for me, too. I'd get extra presents, and not lose things or break things."

Mummy laughed. "Oh, good luck doesn't come to Margery because of her lucky man, though she thinks it does. It comes because she's a careful, thoughtful child, who keeps her things nicely—and it comes because she's generous and kind, so that people want to give her presents. You act the same as Margery, Jack, and things will go right for you, too."

Margery kept her lucky little man on a tiny silver chain round her neck. She only took him off when she washed, and then she was careful not to put him in a place where Jack could find him. Jack was cross and sulky about it. He was more and more determined to get that little lucky man if he could!

When his birthday came, he had a lovely surprise. His Mother and Father gave him a new bicycle! His old one had belonged to his cousin and was very rusty and shabby. When Jack saw his new bicycle he could hardly believe his eyes!

"Oh, Mummy! Daddy! What a wonderful present! *Thank* you!"

"Keep it nice, Jack," said Mummy. "It looks so beautiful now."

"Can I ring the bell, Jack?" asked Margery. She rang it. "Ting-a-ling!" It made a very loud noise indeed. The bicycle had a basket on the front and a saddle-bag full of tools at the back. It really was a beauty.

Jack went for rides on it every day. He kept it very

clean and bright, because he was so proud of it. Then he ran into another boy's bicycle and scratched some of the brightness from it.

"Oh dear! What a bit of bad luck!" said Jack in alarm. "I hope I'm not going to have more bad luck —I'm not a very lucky person, really. Wouldn't it be awful if I smashed up my lovely new bike!"

He was so worried that he went to Margery again. "Margery, I believe I'm going to have a bit of bad luck again. *Please* lend me your little lucky man to put in my saddle-bag, so that I don't spoil my new bicycle."

"No," said Margery. "I never will!"

"Mean thing!" said Jack and went off sulkily. He wondered what Margery did with her little lucky man now. She didn't wear it round her neck any more. The teacher at school had said that no child was to wear necklaces, so Margery had stopped wearing him except at week-ends.

Jack watched to see what Margery did with the little lucky man whilst she was at school. He soon found out! She put him into the little teapot belonging to her dolls' tea-set. That was a very good hiding-place indeed. Jack would never, never have thought of it.

He let Margery go to school before him one morning, and then he ran to the playroom, took out the teapot, and lifted out the little lucky man. He put back the teapot and ran to his bicycle. He must hide that little man somewhere on his bicycle! Somewhere that Margery would never find. Then the little man would bring him luck, and his bicycle wouldn't have silly accidents and be spoilt. Where should he hide it?

Not in the saddle-bag. Margery would certainly look there. Not in the basket. He would be far too easily seen. Where, then?

Jack had a sudden idea. He unscrewed the top off his bell. He put the tiny little lucky man in the bottom of the bell, and then screwed the top on again. He rang the bell.

"Ting-a-ling-a-ling!" Yes, it was quite all right, even with the little man inside it. Aha! Margery would never, never find him now. Jack rode off to school, delighted to think that he would have a little good luck himself because he had got Margery's lucky man.

Well, it certainly was very queer, but things did go very well for Jack that morning. He was top in arithmetic, he got full marks for dictation, and he jumped higher than anyone else at gym. He did feel pleased.

When he got home that morning he told his Mother all about his good luck. Margery looked sharply at him. Then she went to the playroom and took out her dolls' teapot. She looked inside. No lucky man there! She ran to Jack.

"You've taken my lucky man! You horrid, mean boy! Give him back at once. Where is he?"

"Shan't tell you," said Jack. "I'm going to keep him for one whole day. I'll give him back to you to-night. Surely you can spare him just for one day, you mean girl?"

"I know where he is! Somewhere on your bicycle!" cried Margery, suddenly guessing. "I'll find him! I'll find him!"

She ran to Jack's bike. He followed her, feeling quite certain that she would never find the little man. Margery looked in the basket and in the saddle-bag. Jack stood by, grinning broadly. Margery felt very angry indeed. "Well, he won't bring you any luck, so there!" she said, almost crying. "He won't, he won't!"

"He has already—and he'll bring me lots more!" said Jack. And you know, it was very strange, but that afternoon Jack kicked three goals at football, found the shoes he had lost at school the term before, and was asked out to a party the next day. What luck!

On the way home he had to call and get some shoes from the cobbler's for his Mother. He put his bicycle against the outside of the shop and went in. He had to wait whilst the cobbler looked in the rows of mended shoes for his Mother's pair.

And would you believe it—when he got outside again, his bicycle was gone! It simply wasn't there at all. Jack stared at the place where he had left it, but it was quite empty. He went inside the shop and told the cobbler.

"Well, there, now—what a pity!" said the cobbler. "There's a lot of bicycles been stolen this week—two of them from this very street, too. So your lovely new one has gone, has it? What a bit of bad luck!"

Bad luck? It was *dreadful* luck, the worst possible! He had lost his beautiful new bicycle—and goodness knew if he would ever see it again. Those bicycle thieves were so very clever.

Jack went home slowly and sadly, carrying the shoes. He thought of the little lucky man inside the bell. He had gone, too. Margery would never see him again. Oh dear! It seemed as if he had brought bad luck now instead of good.

Margery was very upset and angry. "I told you that you would have bad luck if you took away my little lucky man!" she scolded. "It serves you right! Now your bicycle has gone, and I expect my good luck has too."

"Don't be so angry with poor Jack," said her Mother. "He is very unhappy about his new bicycle. Daddy is ringing up the police to tell them."

But the police did not think they could get back the bicycle for Jack. "You see, sir," they said to Daddy, "these thieves are very, very clever. They'll have painted that bicycle green or red or blue by tonight, taken off the basket and saddle-bag, put on others, and done everything they can to make it look like another bicycle altogether. And even if your boy thinks he can recognise his bicycle under a new coat of paint there's no way of telling it's his."

So Jack had to use his very shabby one again, and he was sad about it. He tried to make things up with Margery by giving her his old Meccano set, but she was very unhappy about her lucky man.

And then something happened. Jack rode over to the next village to see a friend of his, and on the way back he saw a bicycle standing with others in a shed. It was padlocked so that it could not be stolen. It was painted a bright green, and had on a lamp, no basket, and a very old saddle-bag. But something about it made Jack feel absolutely certain that it was his! "I know the look of it! I'm sure it's mine, even though it's green now. Oh dear! How can I possibly know for certain that it's mine?"

He suddenly thought of something. He looked for the bell. Yes, that was still there. Could he unscrew the top and look inside before the owner came out—because the little lucky man might still be there? And if he was, that would prove that the bicycle really was Jack's!

There was no one about. All the men were working in the factory nearby. Jack went up to the green bicycle and began to unscrew the top of the bell. His fingers trembled so that he could hardly take it off.

But at last it was off. Jack looked into the bottom part of the bell—and, yes, the little lucky man *was* there! Jack stared in the greatest delight. Should he take it out? No, because then he would have no proof that the bicycle was his.

He must go to the police station and tell the police there all about it. They could easily telephone the police in the next village where Jack's home was and hear all about how his bicycle was stolen.

So off went Jack to the police station and was soon pouring out his news. The big, stolid policeman listened carefully and wrote down a lot of notes in his notebook. "Thank you, my boy," he said. "Now come with me and show me which is your bicycle."

So off went Jack and pointed out his bicycle. He unscrewed the top of the bell and showed the little lucky man inside. The policeman chuckled. "Aha! The thief didn't think of any one popping a little fellow like that inside the bell! Well, well—it was a lucky thing for you that you put him there."

Jack was told to go home and wait. Nothing could be done till the man came out of the factory and unpadlocked his bicycle. A plain-clothes policeman was going to follow him home and see where he lived and who his friends were.

Jack rushed home and told his mother and Margery all about it. Margery was so thrilled to hear that her little lucky man was inside the bell still that she hugged Jack like a bear. "Oh, if I get him back I'll forgive you for taking him!" she said. "Oh, Jack—it was bad luck that your bicycle was stolen, but very *good* luck that the little man helped you to know it was yours!"

Two policemen arrived that evening, one with Jack's bicycle. "We followed the thief," said one of them. "He didn't go home. He went up on the heath to a deserted hut—and there under a pile of sacks we found three other stolen bicycles he was in the middle of repainting. We've got them all now. We arrested the man, of course. He's a thief we've been looking for for a very long time. Thanks to the sharpness of this boy here we've caught him, and been lucky enough to get back other bicycles for their owners as well!"

Margery watched whilst Jack undid the bell. He took out the lucky man and gave him to her. She was so pleased to have him again.

"He *is* lucky!" she said. "I don't care what anyone says! He helped you to get back your bike, Jack—and he got back three other stolen ones—and gave the police enough good luck to catch the thief. He's a very, very lucky little man!"

Well—he certainly seems to be, doesn't he?'

Adventure in the Afternoon

JACK had a camera. He had had it for his birthday, and he was very pleased with it indeed. It wasn't a new one—it was a very old one, really, that his father had seen in a shop and had bought second-hand.

"New cameras are much too expensive," he told Jack. "And, anyway, it is best to learn on an old one —and this is quite a good one. Here's a little instruction book to go with it—it tells you exactly what to do when you want to take a picture."

Jack was thrilled! A camera! Aha—now he could take his own pictures—and what beauties he would get.

"What are you going to photograph?" said Eileen, his sister. "Will you take me, Jack? I'd like you to take a snap of me."

"Oh *no*," said Jack. "I'm not going to waste my precious films on snapshots of *people*, Eileen. Anybody can do that."

"Well, what are you going to photograph?" said Eileen. "Birds? Animals?"

"No," said Jack. "They won't keep still enough for me. I'm going to take pictures of cars and trains and aeroplanes. I'm going to make my own book of cars, to begin with. I shall photograph every kind of car!

It will be great fun watching out for them and photographing them."

"Yes. That should be good fun," said Eileen. "Are you going to take a picture of our car, Jack? If you do, I could sit at the wheel as if I'm driving it. Do let me."

So Jack took his first picture—and it was of his Father's own car, a Morris, with Eileen sitting up at the wheel as if she were driving it!

He wandered off, with his camera on a strap round his neck. He felt grand with a camera of his own. But he didn't mean to take the things people usually took. No—he was going to take pictures of the things he was most interested in, and those were cars, planes and trains. Ships, too, when he was by the sea.

For the next week Jack had a fine time. He took a picture of a beautiful Rolls Royce car, complete with a very grand chauffeur. He took a picture of a tiny little baby-car with a dog at the back. It had been left there to guard the car, and it barked loudly and fiercely at Jack when he came up with his camera.

"Don't you want your picture taken?" said Jack, and he clicked the camera. "Well—I've taken it! And if you come out on it with your mouth wide open, barking madly, don't blame *me*."

When he had finished the whole film his Father showed him how to develop each picture. Soon Jack had six beautiful pictures of cars to stick into his Car Book. He was very proud and pleased.

"You've really done well with your first film," said his Father in surprise.

"Well, I read that little book of instructions carefully first," said Jack, "and did exactly what it said."

"Sensible of you," said his Father. "Most people rush at a new thing—they don't trouble to learn anything about it first, and then they wonder why they get poor results. You deserve your camera, Jack."

Jack went on with his photographing of all kinds of cars. He got Austins and Bentleys and Rileys and Standards and Rovers and Vauxhalls—in fact, all the cars you see rushing about on the roads each day. I expect you know as many as he did.

He stuck the pictures of them in his book. "I've got nearly every make of car now," he told his Father. "I've got American cars too—and look, that's a French one—and there's another. I haven't got an Italian one yet. There's room for that, if only I can get one. They're lovely cars, aren't they, the big Italian ones?"

His Father didn't know as much about cars as Jack did, and he laughed. "Funny hobby, this, of yours," he said to Jack. "I don't know that it's much use, really; it's fun for you, of course, but, honestly, your book looks rather like a catalogue of second-hand cars."

Jack didn't mind. He enjoyed his hobby, and he loved taking his camera out, ready to snap any new or unusual car that he saw. It was fun to snap them, and even more fun to develop the film and see what kind of picture he had got.

One afternoon he was sitting by the roadside, waiting for cars to come by. There was a lovely view to be seen from the place he had chosen and cars often pulled up to look at it. Then Jack could snap them if they were cars he wanted.

It was very hot indeed. Jack moved out of the sun and snuggled into the greenery of the hedge. His eyes shut. He was asleep!

He was awakened by the sound of a car pulling up near to him. He opened his eyes, yawned and poked his head out of the shady greenery around. Then he sat up straight in delight.

An Italian car! A real beauty—long-bonneted, yellow in colour, with bright silver lines shining here and there. What a car! Just what he wanted for his book of car photographs.

He pulled his camera case over to him and took out his camera. He saw a man get out of the car and walk to the wall on the other side of the road. He had something in his hand, but Jack couldn't see what it was.

To the boy's surprise the man lifted his hand and threw what he was holding over the wall. Then he walked back to the car. "They'll be off again in half a jiffy," thought Jack. "I must snap the car at once or I'll miss it. What a beauty! I shall never see such a fine Italian car again!"

He hurriedly knelt up on one knee and squinted down at the little camera mirror that told him whether the car was in his picture or not. It was—right in the middle, shining beautifully in the sun. The man was just walking over to it.

Click! Jack snapped down the little lever that took the picture, and at the same moment the driver revved up his engine—*rrrrrr-rrrrrr-rrrr!*

The car shot off at top speed. Nobody had spotted Jack in the shade of the hedge. Nobody had heard the click of his camera. How Jack hoped that his picture would come out well! What a beautiful car to add to the collection in his Car Book!

He was walking home, longing to develop his roll of films and see what the picture of the Italian car was like, when he saw a black car coming along in the distance. Jack saw a sign glowing at the top of it:

POLICE

"A police car," he said to himself. "A Wolseley, and jolly fast too, I should think. I wish they'd stop, because I've got just one more picture to take on this film—and although I've got plenty of Wolseleys, I've never had one yet with POLICE showing at the top."

Just as if the car had heard his wish it slowed down and stopped beside him! Jack hurriedly took his camera out of his case. Now—he could snap this police car.

But before he could snap the car, a uniformed policeman put his head out of the window. "Hey, Sonny! Seen any cars along here lately?"

"Only one in the last half-hour," said Jack. "I fell asleep in the hedge."

The policeman gave an exclamation of annoyance. "Well, you won't be much help then. What was the car you saw?"

"An Italian car," said Jack. "It stopped just by me, and the noise of the engine woke me up."

"Ha! Good!" said the policeman. "Then you can tell me who was in the car—how many—and what they were like."

"Oh—no—I can't tell you that," said Jack, trying to think hard. "I didn't notice. I just saw a man get out of the car and throw something over the wall down there—some rubbish, I suppose—and then he got back and the car drove away at once."

"What was the man like?" asked the policeman at once.

"I don't know," said Jack. "I really didn't notice, sir."

"Think of that!" said the policeman in an exasperated voice, turning to another man in the car. "Here's a boy who had a good chance of seeing how many were in the car, what they were like, and everything—and all he knows is what the car looked like!"

Jack felt hurt at the man's tone. "Well, sir, I know you think I'm jolly stupid," he said. "But actually I was photographing the car for my Car Book—so naturally I didn't bother about the people in it."

Then things happened very quickly!

The three policemen in the car exclaimed loudly, one of them hauled Jack into the car, and another whipped his camera case off his shoulder!

"He may have got just what we want!" said one of them. "We'll get the snap developed immediately! Johns, you drop off at the wall where this youngster says he saw one of the men throw something over, and see what you can find. We'll drive on to the police station and get this film developed at once."

"But it's *my* film!" began Jack indignantly. "I always develop my own films. What's all the excitement about?"

"Well, you deserve to know, seeing that it is likely you may be going to present us with a photograph of one or two people who are concerned in a robbery of valuable State papers," said the first policeman. "We've an idea who they are, but we've no proof at the moment. All we know is that they drove off in a big Italian car."

Now it was Jack's turn to get excited! Fancy his camera snapping the very car with the robbers in—and maybe the very robbers themselves. Jack remembered the man who had been walking towards the car just when he had snapped it. Surely he would be in the picture?

One of the policemen dropped off at the wall and jumped over it to see what he could find. He hoped to get the case in which the stolen papers had been kept. It would be empty, of course—but there might be fingerprints on it.

The police car sped on to the big police station in the next town. The film was taken from Jack's camera and was soon being developed in a little dark-room. Jack watched in excitement.

At last one of the policemen gave a whistle and held up the roll of film to the light. "Look here! This is the car—and who's that beside it? It's Lennie Richardson, isn't it? We thought he was in this. And look, here's a man at the wheel, he's come out plainly—my word, it's Pete Lucien!"

"Is it a good snap?" asked Jack, patiently trying to get a peep of it.

"Fine! Couldn't be better!" said the policeman. "What a bit of luck for us! Got the car *and* the men all in one picture—absolutely positive proof of the thieves concerned. Sonny, you did much better than you knew when you snapped that car!"

Well—what a thrill for Jack! The thieves were caught because of his picture, and in the newspapers the next day was the photograph he had taken of the car and the men!

Jack was so proud that he couldn't stop talking about it.

"Fancy my little old camera taking a picture so valuable as that!" he kept saying. "What a fine picture I've got to put in my Car Book—the best and most exciting of the lot."

All the newspapers that printed Jack's car picture

paid him a fee for it—and to his enormous surprise the boy soon had more money than he had ever had in his life!

"Almost ten pounds!" he said. "Well, I know what I'm going to do with it!"

I know too, don't you? He's going to buy a really magnificent camera now, for a Train Book. If ever you meet him, ask him to show you his Car Book—it's really very interesting indeed. *Especially* the last two pictures in the book—a big Italian car, shining in the sun—and a gleaming black car with a word showing clearly at the top—POLICE.

"Isn't He a Coward!"

"You're a coward, Harry!" cried Dick.

"I'm not," said Harry.

"Well, climb up to the top of the school wall and jump down, then," shouted Ronnie.

"I don't want to," said Harry. "I might twist my ankle and then I shouldn't be able to play football tomorrow. I don't see any sense in doing a thing like that."

"Coward!" yelled everyone. Dick climbed to the top of the wall and stood there, balancing cleverly. Then he jumped down.

"Easy!" he said proudly to Harry. "Go on. Do it. I dare you to!"

"Dares are silly," said Harry. "You know they are. If everybody did all they were dared to do there would be an awful lot of broken arms and legs."

"You're afraid," said Mike scornfully. "You say things like that because you are afraid."

"No I don't," said Harry. "I'm not afraid. I've courage enough to stand here and refuse to do something silly which I could quite well do if I tried, haven't I? You wait till there's some real reason for doing things like that and I'll do them. But not just because you dare me to."

"I dare you to jump into the river on the way home!" yelled Mike. "You won't drown because the river isn't deep enough. You just prove you're not a coward, see, and jump into the river!"

"And get soaked just to show you I'm not a coward!" said Harry.

"Cowardy-cowardy-custard!" yelled all the boys and danced round him in delight. "Harry the coward! Coward Harry!"

Harry was tempted to climb to the top of the wall straightaway and jump down, just to show the boys what he thought of them—but he didn't. He *might* just twist his ankle, because the wall was high—and how silly not to be able to play in the football match just because he wanted to show off in front of the boys. Let them think he was a coward if they wanted to. *He* didn't care!

But he *did* care. He cared dreadfully. He hated it when the boys called after him down the street. He couldn't bear it when his Mother heard Dick yelling "Cowardy-cowardy-custard!" after him. He began to wonder if he really was a coward.

"I never have done anything brave," he thought. "I've never rescued anyone from drowning or from a burning house or anything like that. I wonder if I *am* a coward. I do hope I'm not."

One afternoon he took another way home and managed to give the boys the slip. He went down Chestnut Way and walked beside the high wall that ran round Chestnut House. A cross old man lived there, with a crowd of growling dogs. Nobody went into the grounds if they could help it.

Round the corner he came across two people. One was a small girl and she was crying. The older was a big boy, bigger than Harry, from the school at the other end of the town.

"What's the matter?" said Harry to the little girl.

"He's thrown my doll over the wall," wept the child. "It was Amelia, my best doll. She'll be broken. She'll be eaten up by dogs."

"What a horrid thing to do!" said Harry to the big boy. The boy put up his fists at once.

"I'll fight you if you talk like that to me!" he said.

Then there came a noise of voices and footsteps, and round the corner came Harry's school-fellows— Dick, Mike, Ronnie and the rest.

"Here he is!" cried Dick. "Trying to give us the slip. Here's Harry, old cowardy-custard."

"Shut up," said Harry. "Something's happened.
This big lout has thrown this little girl's doll over the
wall. I was just going to fight him."

The boys stared at the big boy, who still had his
fists up. They looked at Harry, who was much smaller.

"I'll take him on after you've finished with him,
Harry," said Dick.

"So will I," said Mike.

The big boy looked scared. "I'm not fighting the whole lot of you," he said—and, quite suddenly, he turned on his heel and fled away as fast as ever he could down the road.

"What did you want to make him do that for, just as I was going to punish him for teasing this little girl?" said Harry crossly to the boys. "He was bigger than me, I know—but I have learnt boxing and I could have beaten him easily."

The little girl gave a sob. "I don't like boys to fight," she said. "I want my doll."

The boys looked up at the high wall. "It's jolly high," said Mike. "Be difficult to get up—and *I* shouldn't like to jump down the other side. I'd be afraid I couldn't get back."

"And those dogs might come rushing up," said Dick. "And that fierce old man might come along."

The little girl wiped her eyes and looked very miserable. "Goodbye!" she suddenly called to her doll over the wall. "Good-bye, Amelia. I can't get you."

Then she suddenly burst into tears again. Harry put his arm round her.

"Don't you cry," he said. "I've got a little sister at home just like you—and I've often rescued her dolls for her. I'll get yours. Don't worry!"

"Oh, *will* you?" cried the little girl, and she smiled up at Harry. "But how can you?"

"You just see!" said Harry. He ran a little way up the road to where a tree leaned over the wall. He was up that tree in a trice.

"What are you going to do?" cried Dick. "You can't jump down the other side, idiot. You'd never get back. And those dogs are always about."

"Well, you come and do it, then," said Harry. But nobody wanted to.

They all stood and watched Harry swing himself on to the top of the wall.

The boy looked down the other side. It was a big jump. Bigger than from the top of the school wall. Suppose he broke his ankle?

Well, he wouldn't. He wasn't going to disappoint the little girl now that he had said he would get her doll. He swung himself down from the wall and landed on the ground. He fell into the soft earth and gave himself only a slight jolt.

The other boys swarmed up the tree that Harry had climbed, and they sat on the top of the wall to watch him. The boy looked for the doll. Ah, there it was, caught in a bush. He went over to get it.

Suddenly, not far off, he heard a bark. Golly, the dogs were about, then! He snatched at the doll.

But before he could get back to the wall and get the other boys to drag him up, a big dog came running round the bushes. He saw Harry and growled. He bared his big teeth.

The boy began to back towards the wall. The dog growled so fiercely that he stopped. The boys on the wall held their breath. Surely the big dog would not fly at Harry?

"What's happening? Oh, what's happening?" cried the little girl, who was on the path outside the wall.

"Is that one of the dogs growling at Harry?"

"There are two dogs now—no, three!" said Dick, and stared down from the wall in horror. "Harry—make a dash for it. We'll help you up. Don't be afraid."

"I'm not afraid," said Harry. "But I know jolly well if I *do* make a dash for the wall the dogs will be on me. I must try to make friends with them, that's all." He boldly held out his hand to the nearest dog.

"Good dog," he said. "Good dog. Fine fellow."

The dog growled, but not so fiercely as before. Harry still held out his hand, then the dog sniffed at it. "Good dog!" said Harry again. "Fine fellow!"

The dog turned his back on Harry as if he was no longer interested in him. Harry stretched out his hand to the second dog. "Good dog!" he began again. "I'm a friend. A friend, see? And you're a good dog!"

The dog growled. Then he put back his head and

barked loudly. Dick almost fell off the wall in sudden fright.

Harry made a move towards the wall. But the second and third dogs came close to him at once, growling. It was plain that they were not going to allow him to escape. Harry looked at them in despair. He couldn't stay there all day! But what was he to do?

The dogs suddenly pricked up their ears and turned their heads. The boys heard a deep voice calling.

"What's the matter with you, Boris? Why are you barking, Leo? Come here, Scamp, and stop your noise."

"It's the old man," whispered Dick to Mike. "Now poor old Harry's properly caught. Let's go while there's time."

"That would be cowardly," said Mike at once. "We must stay and stick by Harry."

A man came round the bushes. He had thick black hair streaked with silver and shaggy black eyebrows that looked very fierce. He frowned when he saw Harry standing there.

"So you came into my grounds and the dogs found you, did they?" he demanded. "And what were you doing here, I'd like to know? Come after my plums?"

"No, sir," said Harry. "I wouldn't dream of such a thing."

The man looked at him closely. "I've seen you before," he said. "Aren't you the boy that the others call 'Cowardy-cowardy-custard' when you go down the road?"

"Yes, sir," said Harry, going red. "But I'm not a coward."

A clear little voice came over the wall. It was the little girl speaking. "He's brave! A big boy threw my doll Amelia over your wall—and Harry went to fetch her. He isn't a coward, he's brave. Please don't let your dogs hurt him."

The old man saw the doll under Harry's arm. He saw the row of boys sitting on the wall, looking rather ashamed.

"So," he said to Harry, "you, the boy that the others shout after, are the one that jumps down into the grounds where you know there are dogs, to get a little girl's doll. And the others sit up there in safety. Cowards, all of them! Bah! You're worth a hundred of them. Throw the little girl's doll over to her and come and have tea with me. I've got plenty of things a boy like you would like to see."

"Well, thanks very much, sir—but I'd rather go with the others, if you don't mind," said Harry. "They're not cowards, sir—they've often done things they've dared me to do. I'm not a coward either, but they thought I was."

"Well, you're not, Harry. You're braver than any of us!" shouted down Mike. "And more sensible, too. You only do daring things when there's a real reason for them—we did them just for a silly show-off. We'll never call you coward again!"

"Well said!" cried the old man. "Good boy! I'll tell you what we'll do. Harry can go off with you today, but you can *all* come to tea with me tomorrow—yes, and make friends with my dogs, too. Now, over the wall you go, Harry—and I'll see you all tomorrow!"

And up the wall and over he went, dropping lightly down to the other side.

"Good-bye, sir, and thank you!" Harry called. Then the others dropped down beside him. Mike thumped him on the back.

"Sorry we were such idiots about you, Harry," he said. "Be friends with us. We'll be proud."

"Course I will," said Harry. "You just didn't know, that's all. Hallo, here's the little girl again. Come along, youngster, we'll take you and Amelia safely home, and if you ever see that big boy again, you tell him Harry will be after him if he teases you any more!"

Then off they went together, laughing and shouting —but the happiest of them all was Harry. He wasn't a coward—and everybody knew it. Hurrah!

When Mac was a Shadow

MAC LIVED in a big town. It took a long time to get away from it and out into the country, so Mac used to go to the park to play.

"But you can't really play games like Red Indians in the park," he said to the others. "I mean—people wouldn't like us wriggling through the bushes, stalking one another. But it would be such fun to do things like that."

"Red Indians are babyish," said Fred, a big boy. "It's more fun to play at shadowing, or something like that."

"What's shadowing?" asked Mac. "It sounds good."

"Well—it's what the police do sometimes when they want to watch a man they suspect of something," said Fred. "They tell a man to follow him around— act like a shadow—always there, but never noticed."

Mac thought about it. Shadowing could really be done anywhere. It might be fun. He asked Fred another question.

"Do you get into trouble if you shadow people for nothing—just for fun, I mean?"

"Not if you're a good shadower!" said Fred with

a laugh. "They wouldn't even know you were there. Why—are you thinking of trying it?"

"I might," said Mac. "I shall think about it. It might make up for not playing Red Indians."

He did think about it, and he felt rather excited. Yes—it *would* be rather fun to pretend to be a policeman in plain clothes, and shadow someone—someone who wouldn't even guess that he, Mac, was behind him, watching where he went and what he did. He could pretend the man was an escaped prisoner or something.

So after tea the next evening Mac slipped out by himself. He went into the town and looked round for someone to shadow. "I'll choose a nasty-looking fellow who *might* be somebody bad," he thought. "And I must be very, very careful that he doesn't spot me. If he does, he's won and I've lost. We'll both be playing a game together, but he won't know he is!"

75

He wandered along the street, keeping his eyes open for a shifty-looking fellow. But everyone seemed to have a pleasant, kindly face. He stood himself outside a shop and watched.

Somebody came out of the shop and bumped into Mac. "Oh, sorry," he said. "I didn't see you there."

Mac rubbed his knee, where the man's heavy bag had knocked it. "It's all right," he said, and wondered if he should shadow this man. But he looked so jolly and friendly that Mac felt sure he wasn't anyone bad. So he let the man go and he was soon lost to sight.

Then someone else came by—and Mac decided at once that here was a man to shadow. What a nasty-looking fellow! He looked dirty, his hat was pulled well over his face, a cigarette hung from the side of his mouth, and he slouched along with his hands in his pockets.

"Of course, he won't really be a bad lot at all," thought Mac, "but he looks one, so I'll shadow him."

The man slouched down the street. Mac slipped out of the doorway he stood in and walked after him. The man walked to the corner and turned it. Then he went into a doorway and stood looking at some books there. Mac slipped into another doorway some way behind him and watched to see what the man would do next. Probably go into the shop and buy a book! But he didn't.

He set off again at a fair pace, and then, just as Mac came to the bookshop where the man had stood, the fellow stopped again and looked hard into another window. Mac slid into the doorway of the bookshop and looked at the shelf of books he had seen the man staring at.

He was very surprised when he saw them. They didn't seem at all the kind of books a man like that would study. They were a set of very expensive nature books.

"Oh, well—maybe he's interested in nature," thought Mac, and slipped out of the doorway as he saw the man walking on again.

It was a curious walk that the man took him—a walk that was interrupted by many starings into shop windows, and standing in doorways, looking out. Mac began to feel puzzled. Surely the man didn't know he was following him?

And then, with quite a shock, Mac noticed what the man was doing. *He* was shadowing someone, too! He was following warily, slipping into doorways when the other man stopped to speak to someone, looking into windows if the other stopped to look at something, too. Mac strained his eyes in the half darkness to try and see what he was like.

"He's carrying a bag," he thought. "Why—it's the man who came out of that shop and bumped into me. His bag felt very heavy when it knocked my knee. Maybe there was money in it—men's wages or something!"

On went the man with the bag—on went the nasty fellow following him—and on went Mac, following too! But now it didn't seem a game any more.

What was the shadower going to do? Was he going to jump on the man with the bag when he came to a dark place, and knock him down, and steal his bag? Mac felt quite sure something horrid was going to happen.

His heart began to beat fast. What could he do? He couldn't possibly stop the man—but neither could he warn the man with the bag! "I must do something, I really must," thought Mac desperately.

And then he saw Fred! He beckoned to him urgently.

Fred joined him in surprise. "I say, Fred," began Mac, in rather a breathless voice. "You'll have to help me. I came out to have a game of shadowing someone —like you told me, you know—and I chose that horrid-looking fellow, some way in front there, to follow. Do you see him? Well—I've now discovered that *he's* shadowing someone, too—a man with a bag that I'm sure is full of money."

"Golly!" said Fred. "And he's going to knock him on the head when he comes to a dark spot!"

"Yes, I'm sure he is," said Mac. "So look here, Fred —you rush off now and find a policeman and tell him what is happening. It's no good telling the man with the bag, he might just laugh. The policeman will know what to do."

"Right," said Fred, and darted off up the street, passing the shadower and the man with the bag, too. He was soon out of sight, trying to find a policeman.

The man with the bag now walked steadily on. He met no one because he was now in a more deserted part of the town. He turned down a dark lane.

Immediately the shadower hurried a little and

began to close in. Mac hurried, too, his heart thumping. The shadower was now almost up to the first man, and Mac saw him raise his arm. Mac yelled loudly as the man with the bag dodged and fell to the ground. He hung on to his bag, though the shadower was tugging hard at it.

And then Fred appeared with a burly policeman! Oh, what a relief! Mac, Fred and the policeman surrounded the surprised thief. The man on the ground got up and dusted himself down. He was feeling dazed—but he still had his bag of money firmly clutched in his hand.

Things happened quickly after that. The thief was arrested at once, and the policeman asked Fred, Mac and the man with the bag to come along, too.

"Good boy, you," said the policeman to Fred. "Fetched me along just in the nick of time!"

"Oh, it was Mac here who sent me to find you," said Fred. "He was shadowing the shadower, and guessed what was going to happen."

Everyone was most astonished to hear this, especially the thief. "What? You were behind me all the time?" he growled. "What for?"

"Well—just for a game, actually," said Mac. "And then it suddenly changed from a game to the real thing."

"What a bit of luck for me!" said the man with the bag, who was now quite recovered. He patted Mac on the back. "Funny sort of thing to do, though— follow a man you don't know, just for a game. Are you going to be a policeman or a detective or something when you grow up?"

"Well—I might," said Mac, suddenly thinking that it might be a very good idea.

What a hero Mac was at school the next day! The boys crowded round to hear the story, and even the headmaster congratulated him on his queer adventure. And nicest of all was the reward that came to him from the man with the bag.

"Ten whole pounds!" said Mac, hardly believing his eyes. "Ten whole pounds! Well—no more shadowing for me—I'm going to buy a bike with this and ride out into the country each Saturday—and I'm going to play Red Indians there, and go stalking through the fields and hedges."

"Well, mind you don't stalk a bull, young Mac!" said Fred. "I shan't be there to fetch a policeman for you next time, you know!"

Sailor Jim's Telescope

SAILOR JIM had a telescope. He put it on a stand down by the sea-wall, and anyone could have a look through it for a penny.

"We can see the lighthouse as if it was as near as the sea-wall!" said Peter.

"And you can see that bird far out to sea just as if it was flying by your nose!" said Lucy.

"And if I look at that far-off boat I can even see who's in it!" said James. "It's my cousin Harry and his friend Don!"

Sailor Jim liked the children. He gave them a free peep through his telescope every Saturday morning if they could come and tell him that they had had good marks at school.

And one day George came to tell him a very fine piece of news indeed. "Sailor Jim—what do you think!" he said. "I've won a scholarship!"

"You don't mean it!" said Sailor Jim. "Well, well, what brains you must have! Now you tell me what you'd like from me for a reward, and you can have it! A sail in my boat? A fishing-trip with me? What would you like to have?"

"Sailor Jim, I suppose you wouldn't lend me your telescope for just one day, would you?" asked George. "My little sister's ill in bed, and she would so love to have your telescope to look through for a little while. She isn't allowed to read. She could look at the birds in the trees, and the sheep far away on the hill—she'd love that!"

"But I wanted to give *you* a reward, not your sister," said Sailor Jim. "Surely you would like to go on a fishing-trip with me, George?"

"Oh, *yes*—better than anything," said George. "But I know how Pat would like your telescope for just one day. She's often said so."

Sailor Jim didn't know what to say. He really didn't want to part with his telescope for a whole day, especially as there were many people visiting his town now—he would lose a lot of pennies. But still, he had said that George could ask for what he wanted.

"Right," he said at last. "You can take it to-morrow. But be careful of it, won't you?"

George was delighted. How pleased Pat would be! She would feel better at once.

He called for it the next morning and proudly took it off to his sister. She squealed with delight when she saw it and held out her hands. Soon it was propped up on her bed, and she was looking through it.

"The sheep look so big!" she said. "And now I can see the two little foals properly in the next field. And I can see the rooks pecking up grubs and the shepherd's dog scratching himself. It's like magic! Everything is so near!"

After tea her mother left her by herself with the telescope. George was out in the garden reading. Pat settled down to look through the telescope. She turned it on Mr. Land's farm and watched the hens and the ducks there. She turned it on the big field and saw the cows walking through the gate to be milked.

"And now I'll look at that dear little thatched cottage," she said to herself. The cottage was near the railway line, and trains often went by. Pat could watch the trains with the telescope as well as have a look at the cottage, with its thatched roof and tall hollyhocks.

"It's rather like a fairy-tale cottage," she thought.

"I wonder where the old lady is who lives there? Perhaps she is still having her tea indoors. Oh—here comes a train!"

She heard the rumble and then saw the smoke from the engine. The train went tearing by the cottage, spitting out smoke and a trail of sparks from its funnel.

It soon disappeared. Pat looked at the cottage through the telescope again. She saw something on the thatched roof. What could it be?

It moved about. Was it a white bird? No—it couldn't be. It grew bigger. It was—yes, it must be —smoke!

"*Smoke!*" said Pat in alarm. "Smoke on the old cottage's thatched roof! A spark from the engine must have blown there—and it's set light to the dry thatch—the straw has caught alight. Oh dear—the cottage will be burnt down!" The little girl raised her voice and shouted: "Mummy! MUMMY! Quick, come here!"

Her mother and George came running up at once. "Look," cried Pat, pointing out of the window. "A spark has set the roof of that cottage on fire. It's burning. Call the fire-engine, quick! I saw it through the telescope George brought me."

Mummy flew downstairs to the telephone. She got on to the fire-station at once and told them her news.

"Thanks, madam. The old thatched cottage near the railway, you say? We'll be there in three minutes!"

And so they were! Pat watched the whole thing through the telescope in the greatest excitement.

The fire-engine raced up. The firemen leapt down. A hose was unrolled, and water began to play on the burning thatch. And in the middle of it all an old lady came angrily out of her cottage.

"What are you doing? What is the meaning of this?" she cried. The firemen pointed to the smoking roof where the flames were now almost out.

"Your roof was on fire, missus," said one. "Just got the warning in time."

"Who gave the warning?" said the old lady, astonished.

"A little girl called Pat, who lives up in that house over there," said the fireman, pointing. "She told her mother and her mother telephoned through to us—and here we are!"

"Thank you, thank you," said the old lady. "I must tell my son, and he will go and thank the little girl."

Who do you suppose her son was? *Sailor Jim.* Wasn't that strange? He was so glad to know that his mother's cottage had been saved that he walked up to George's house that evening and asked to see Pat.

"I'd like to see the little girl who noticed that my mother's roof was on fire," he said to Pat's mother. "I want to thank her."

So up he went into Pat's bedroom—and the very first thing he saw there was his own telescope! He stared at it in astonishment.

"How did you get this?" he asked, picking it up.

"George brought it home for just one day for me to look through—my brother George," said Pat. "And it was when I was looking through it after tea that I saw the roof of that cottage smoking. Wasn't it a good thing I had the telescope?"

"It was," said Sailor Jim. "A very good thing indeed. And what a very, *very* good thing I lent it to George because he won a scholarship!"

"Oh! Are you Sailor Jim?" cried Pat. "George, George, come quickly, here's Sailor Jim!"

George came in and looked astonished to see Sailor Jim. "Have you come for the telescope?" he asked.

"George, it was Sailor Jim's mother's cottage I saw burning through *his* telescope!" cried Pat. "Isn't it queer—just like a house-that-Jack-built story!"

Sailor Jim laughed. "This is the boy who won a scholarship. This is the man who wanted to give him a reward. This is the telescope he lent him. This is the little girl who used it. That's the cottage she saw burning—and here's the man who came to say thank you for saving his mother's home."

"Oh, Sailor Jim—I'm glad your telescope saved your mother," said George. "What a good thing I asked for it!"

"Yes—and I'm giving you something else now," said Sailor Jim. "Another reward! Will you both come out fishing with me as soon as this little lady is better?"

"I'll be better to-morrow. I will! I will!" cried Pat.

"You get better by next Saturday and we'll go," said Sailor Jim. So Pat is going to get well by then, and off they will all go together to catch plenty of fish for Saturday's supper.

It's queer how things happen, isn't it? You simply never know!

Adventure for Two

"COMING with me in the car?" called Daddy to Jack and Mary. "I'm just going down to see old Mrs. Blakey."

"Oh, is she ill?" said Mary. Her daddy was a doctor and went to see ill people every day.

"No, not ill. She's sprained her ankle, that's all," said Daddy. "I'm just going to have a look at it—and then I rather thought I'd go to the bakery and have one of those chocolate ice-creams of theirs. But you know how I hate eating ice-creams alone."

"Oooh, Daddy! Of course we'll come!" said Jack. He came running out of the playroom with Mary. "You're a brick, Daddy! You always tell us when you're going ice-creaming!"

They went to get their hats and coats. Their father went out to get his car. He brought it into the front drive.

Jack and Mary came running out. "I'll go in the front now, and you can be there coming back," said Mary to Jack. In they got, and off went the car. Down the drive, out into the road, and up the hill. Down the hill and round the corner—and there was old Mrs. Blakey's house, with its thick yew hedge all round the front garden.

"Now you just look after my car for me whilst I'm in the house," said Daddy, "then I shan't need to lock it up. I always have to if there's nobody in it, because my precious case of medicines might be stolen."

"Oh, yes," said Jack. "And some of them are very poisonous, aren't they?"

Daddy went up the path to the house. The children sat in the car, looking at the thick yew hedge. Mary got out.

"I just want to look at the hedge," she said to Jack. "It's so very, very thick. Why, it's thick enough to get right into the middle of it!"

Jack got out, too. They had always liked old Mrs. Blakey's thick yew hedge. Mary parted the green boughs and looked into the depths of the dark hedge.

"Jack!" she said. "Look! There's a kind of passage going right along the middle of the hedge!"

Jack looked. It did really seem like a passage! The leaves there had dried and fallen off, and the middle of the hedge was empty and bare.

"We could almost go along it," said Jack. "Mary—shall we just get into it for a minute? I believe if we were in the very middle nobody could possibly see us! What a wonderful hiding-place it would make!"

"Let's hide from Daddy!" said Mary at once. "That *would* be fun! He'd come out and look for us—and we wouldn't be there!"

"And we could say something in a very deep, hollow kind of voice," said Jack. "It would make him jump! Come on, Mary, before he comes out."

It was easy to squeeze into the thick yew hedge. Once in the centre the branches closed firmly round them, and nobody could see them.

"But I've got a fine peep-hole, Mary—have you?" asked Jack. "I can see Daddy's car through it."

"Yes. I've got a peep-hole, too—between some leaves," said Mary. "Jack—supposing somebody comes by—had we better keep still and quiet?"

"Yes," said Jack. "We can't give our hiding-place away!"

"I can hear someone coming now," said Mary, and she looked through her peep-hole. "It's Jimmy White!"

Jimmy passed by, whistling cheerfully. Jack and Mary giggled. They longed to say "Beware, Jimmy!" in a deep, peculiar voice, but they knew Jimmy well enough to know that he would at once go to look in the hedge for the voice!

"Now there's a woman coming," whispered Jack. "I don't know her."

The woman passed, walking quickly. The children sat quite still in their hiding-place. The passer-by didn't know anyone was so near her!

Nobody came for a little while. Then Jack heard soft footsteps. He peeped out.

"Two men, Mary," he whispered. "Aren't they walking quietly!"

The men came up to the car—but they didn't walk past. They stopped just by it. The children held their breath in case their hiding-place should be discovered.

"No one about," said one man in a very low voice. "Whose car's this? It's got a case inside."

"It's Doctor Fenton's car," said the other man in such a low voice that the children could hardly hear him. "That will be his case. There will be valuable drugs in there. Any chance of getting them?"

"Better try now, whilst there's no one to see," said the first man. He wrenched the front door of the car open and put his hand in quickly. In a trice he had taken the case and had shut the door quietly.

Then the two men moved off quickly, walking very softly.

The children had seen all this, and were absolutely thunderstruck. Two robbers! Thieves who had dared to open their father's car and take his case—in full daylight, too! Well, you read of such things in the newspapers—but they never, never happened under your nose like this!

"Mary!" said Jack, finding his tongue at last. "We didn't do a thing. We never even shouted."

"I couldn't," said Mary. "It all happened so quickly. What are we going to do? Daddy's case is gone."

"And we were supposed to be in charge of it," said Jack, horrified at the thought. "Goodness—we were pretty feeble, Mary. If only we'd just given one shout those men would have shot off at once, without even opening the car."

"Yes, but it all happened so *quickly*," said Mary, almost in tears. "I couldn't say a word. I did try, but I couldn't. Let's get out of this hedge and tell Daddy."

At that very moment they heard the front door slam, and their father came briskly down the path.

"Now what about our ice-creams?" he called, as he got to the gate.

Jack and Mary were just climbing out of the hedge. They looked untidy and were covered with little bits and pieces. They looked so very solemn that their father was surprised.

"I say—did you *have* to climb into that dirty old hedge?" he said, opening his car. Then he stopped and stared. "Good gracious—where's my case gone?"

"Daddy, it's been stolen," said Jack. "Oh, Daddy, it was our fault. We were in the hedge when the men came by and we . . ."

"Now begin at the beginning and tell me everything," said Daddy, seeing at once that something serious had happened. So the two children told him everything: how they had got into the hedge, how people had come by, and the two men had come and talked, and then had stolen the case.

"Did they see you?" asked Daddy. "Did they know you were there?"

"Oh no," said Jack. "But we saw *them* all right. We know exactly what they are like and how they are dressed. If we saw them again we'd know them."

"Very well, then—hop quickly into the car," said Daddy. "I'll go to the police-station and collect a policeman in plain clothes, and we'll drive slowly round and about the streets. Maybe we'll see those men again!"

This was all very exciting indeed. The children got into the car, and Daddy drove off. He went first to the police-station, told very shortly what had happened, and was given an extra passenger—a burly policeman dressed in ordinary clothes.

"They'll have wrapped up that case of yours in brown paper now, sir," said the policeman. "No good looking for the case—have to look for a large brown-paper parcel, or a suitcase big enough to have put your case in. They wouldn't be foolish enough to carry your bag openly for long. Good thing these youngsters of yours noticed what the men were like!"

The car drove slowly down one street and up another. "There are two men," said the policeman suddenly. "Sitting on that seat, sir; look—with a big parcel."

"No—that's not the men," said Jack. "Is it, Mary? Our men had different clothes—one was in a brown suit with a brown tie, and the other was in a green coat with a black tie."

"Right. Go on again, sir, please," said the policeman. "Ah, wait—what about these men coming round the corner with a case?"

The men had on the right-coloured suits, but they were not a bit like the ones the children had seen.

"No—both those men are small," said Mary, "and our men are tall. One had a little moustache and the other hadn't. And they both wore hats like Daddy's, and one man had a tiny feather stuck into his hat-band."

"My word—these kids of yours notice a lot, don't they?" said the policeman, most impressed. "They'll be telling us how many toes the men had next!"

The children laughed. They were keeping a very close look-out indeed. They had felt so ashamed of letting those men steal their father's case under their very noses; now they felt they really must catch them and get the case back, or they would never forgive themselves.

Up the hill and down. No men at all. Round the town and back again. Plenty of men, but not the ones they wanted.

"Of course they might have gone into a shop somewhere, or the cinema," said the policeman. "They've had time to get a good way away now, and unless they caught a bus or a train they'll probably be sitting down having tea somewhere—or seeing a film. I'm afraid we'll have to give up finding them this way, sir. I've got all particulars from the children—though I'd like to ask them a few questions—and we'll send out descriptions of the men everywhere."

"Right," said Dr. Fenton. "Well, would you like to come along to my house and ask the children what else you want to know?"

Mary spoke up in a very small voice:

"Daddy, I suppose we don't deserve those ice-creams now, do we?"

"Bless us all!" said Daddy. "I'd quite forgotten we were going to have some. Yes, of course we'll have them. Constable, will you join us? You can ask your questions in the bakery."

"Yes, sir. It would be quite a treat," said the policeman, beaming round at the two children. "It's a long time since I was taken out to have an ice-cream."

They came to the bakery, and they got out. This time Daddy locked his car well and truly. "Though it's rather like locking the stable door after the horse has gone," he told the children. "Come along."

They went into the tea-room of the bakery, but it was tea-time now and the place was full. "I've a little room upstairs," said the shop-woman. "I think there's a table up there, sir."

So up they went and found the table. A girl came to take their order. Whilst they were waiting for their ice-creams the two children looked round the room. They had never been in this little room before, and they didn't think it was as nice as the big one downstairs. Still, the ice-creams would be just as good!

Mary suddenly trod hard on Jack's toe. Jack looked at her in surprise. Then he looked where she was looking, and he went bright red with excitement.

Sitting huddled together in the darkest corner of the little room were the two men who had stolen their father's case! There was no mistaking them at all—one with a little moustache, one with none; one with a green coat and black tie, and the other in brown with a brown tie.

And under the table was a very large suitcase! They looked at one another. They didn't dare to whisper their news in case the men suspected something. So Jack took out his little notebook and pencil and scribbled something in it. He passed it silently to his father.

"*Those are the men over there. Look at the suitcase under the table!*" That was what he had written.

His father passed the note to the policeman, who lighted a cigarette and looked casually over at the two men as he did so. He in turn scribbled a note very quickly and had it ready for the girl when she came with their ice-creams. His note was short and clear.

"*Take this to the police-station*," was written on the outside. And inside: "*Send two men to Harrison's Bakery at once. Upstairs. Johns.*"

The girl brought their ice-creams, took the note, looked at the outside, seemed very scared, and went out quietly. Two other people finished their tea and went. That left only the two men and the children's table.

The girl came back and slid a note into the policeman's hands. One of the two men called out to her.

"Hey, miss—what times does the bus to Highlands go?"

"Not for fifteen minutes, sir," said the girl.

"Good," thought the children. "The men won't slip out yet."

Two strange men came into the tea-room and sat down silently at the table next to the children's. They nodded to the policeman, who at once got up and went over to the two men.

"I have reason to think that there is stolen property in that bag of yours," he said. "Will you open it?"

The men leapt up at once, blustering angrily. One caught up the case. "What cheek!" he said. "Who are you to say things like that! I'll report you to the police."

"I *am* the police," said the policeman stolidly. "Open that bag, please."

The men pushed him aside and went to the door. But the other two policemen were there now. No escape that way!

"Huh! Three of you!" said one of the men in

disgust. "All right. Open the case. Though how you know it was us that did the job I don't know. There wasn't anyone to see."

"Walls have ears," said the policeman, opening the bag and taking out Doctor Fenton's bag from inside. "And hedges have eyes!"

Well, of course, the two men had no idea what he was talking about, but the children knew! They were pleased to see the two men marched off.

"I'm glad you've got your bag back, Daddy," said Mary. "We were silly to let it be stolen. What a good thing we came here for ice-creams!"

"It was," said Daddy. "I say—what about another one each just to celebrate your exciting adventure!"

The Secret Door

"WE SHALL be dreadfully bored, staying with Great-Aunt Hannah," said Dick gloomily. "She's nice and kind—but there's absolutely nothing to do at Westroofs."

"What's the house like?" asked Lucy. "You've been there, Dick—Robin and I haven't."

"Well, it's awfully old—and rather dark inside—and there's a big room called the library, which is lined from floor to ceiling with the dullest books you ever saw—and at night the ivy taps on the window-pane and makes you jump!" said Dick.

"Here we are!" said Robin, peering out of the car window as they swung through a pair of enormous old gates. "My word—it *is* an old house—look at the ivy covering it from roof to ground."

Aunt Hannah was waiting to welcome them. She was a dear old lady, with snow-white hair, pink cheeks, and a very kind smile.

"Welcome to Westroofs!" she said. "I do so hope you won't find it dull, my dears. But when I heard that your mother was ill, I really thought it would be a kindness to her to have you here for a while."

The three children felt sure that they would be very dull indeed at Westroofs. There were no horses to ride, no dogs to take for a walk, and not even a cat with kittens to play with. Still, if only the weather was fine, they could go for walks and explore the country round.

But the weather wasn't fine. When they awoke the next morning the rain was pouring down, and it went on all day long. The children roamed about the house, not daring to play any exciting games in case they disturbed Aunt Hannah, who jumped at any sudden shout or stamping of feet.

Next day it was still raining, and the children felt quite desperate. "I've never been so bored in my life," groaned Dick. "Whatever can we do? Let's go out in the rain."

But Aunt Hannah was afraid they would get wet and catch cold. "No, don't go out," she said. "Wouldn't you like to go and look at the books in the library? There are some that belonged to my great-grandfather when he lived at Westroofs. Very, very interesting."

The children didn't feel as if Aunt Hannah's great-grandfather's books would be at all interesting, but they were much too polite to say so. They went into the big, dark library and switched on the middle light, for it was a very dull day.

"There must be hundreds and hundreds of books here that nobody ever reads or wants to read," said Dick, looking at the crowded, dusty shelves. "Here's one that I'm sure nobody has ever read—'History of Edward Lucian, born 1762, in the parish of Elham!' Why, half the pages are still uncut. Poor Edward Lucian!"

"Lucian is our family name. Perhaps he was a great-great-great-ancestor of ours," said Robin. "Look, here's a ladder in this corner. Whatever is it for?"

"To climb up to the topmost shelves I should think, if anyone should ever want a book from there," said Lucy. "Let's put it up. We'll see what kind of books they kept on the top shelf. Do you suppose there are any story-books at all?"

"Shouldn't think so," said Robin, putting the ladder up by the shelves of books. "Well, here I go. If I see anything exciting, I'll toss it down."

Up he went. The top shelf was covered with thick

grey dust. It flew into the air as Robin pulled out one or two books and made him sneeze. The sneeze made him drop a book, and it almost fell on Lucy's head.

"Look out, idiot!" said Lucy, as the book crashed to the floor. It fell half-open, and something flew out of the pages.

"There! One of the pages has got loose," said Lucy. "I'll put it back in its right place."

But when she picked it up, she saw that it was not a loose page but an old, old letter, written on a half-sheet of paper in curious old-fashioned writing. She could hardly make out a word of what it said. She held it out to Dick.

"Look at this old letter," she said. "All the s's are f's. It's impossible to read."

Robin came down the ladder. He too looked at the queer letter. He and Dick began to spell it out slowly.

" 'To-day—I went through—the Secret Door. I have hid my new top there, and the stick I cut from the hedge. William shall not have them. He knows not the way through—through—the Secret Door. He is not—not—allowed in the Sad—Sad'—what *is* this word?—oh, '*Saddle*'. 'He is not allowed in the Saddle Room, and knows not the Secret Panel there'."

The writing ended at that point. The three children were suddenly seized with a great excitement. They stared at one another, feeling rather breathless.

"It's not a letter—it must be part of a diary or something—kept by someone—a boy—who lived here years and years ago!"

"And he had a brother called William. And William didn't know about a secret panel in the saddle-room, or about a secret door. Golly! Let's go and explore! *We* might find them!"

"Where's the saddle-room? Oh, I know—it's the little room at the side of the house, near where the old stables used to be. And it's got panelling all round the walls, I remember! Quick, let's go!"

Forgetting all about putting the ladder back in its corner, or the book back in its place, the children ran out of the dark library, down long passages, and came to the saddle-room.

It was a low, dark room, set round with squared oak panels. Even now there were two or three old saddles

hanging on nails, and a crop lay on a shelf. The rest
of the room contained chairs and tables turned out
from other rooms. It was plainly a kind of store-room
now.

"Now—which would be the secret panel?" said
Dick, looking round the walls. "Golly, isn't this
exciting? Where shall we try first? Not on that wall,
because it's almost covered by that big old picture.
Let's try over here by the fireplace."

"How do we look for a secret panel, and what does
it do?" asked Lucy. "Do we press or push or what?"

"A secret panel was usually put into a wall of
panelling to conceal a cupboard, or some sort of secret
way out or in," said Dick. "We must press each one,
and jiggle it, and see if we can make one move."

Dick began to knock round the walls. "Thud, thud,
thud."

"I might hear if one panel sounds hollow," he said.
"If it did, I'd know it might be the secret one."

But none of them sounded hollow. It was most
disappointing. "Perhaps the panel is behind that big
picture after all," said Dick. "Let's move it."

But they couldn't. It was much too heavy. They
gazed round the little room in despair. Then Dick
went to where a saddle hung on a great nail, and took
it down. "I haven't tried *this* panel," he said, and
knocked on it. It sounded hollow!

"It must be the one!" cried Lucy, and they all
pushed at the brown, polished panel, and banged on
it. But nothing happened. In desperation Dick caught
hold of the big nail and pulled at it.

And then, before their eyes, the panel slid downwards a little, and then sideways, quite soundlessly. Behind it was a dark space. The children stared breathlessly.

"We've found it! We've found the secret panel. What's in the hole?"

Dick sped off for his torch, and soon the children were peering into the hole left by the sliding panel. There didn't seem anything to see at all—just a hole, dark and empty.

"Well—if that isn't disappointing!" said Robin. "Just a hole. And anyway, where's the secret door we read about?" There's no door here. Nobody could get through this hole."

Dick put his hand right into the dark hole and groped round. His hand suddenly found what seemed to be a handle or knob of some kind. He pulled it.

Behind the children came a sudden grating noise, then a terrific crash. They all jumped violently, very frightened. They looked round, scared.

"It's that big picture. It fell off the wall," said Dick. "And, my goodness—look—there's a space behind it. It's the secret door!"

The children stared in delight. There was an opening in the panelling where the great picture had been, an opening big enough to get through! Where did it lead to?

"When I pulled that knob in the hole here it must have worked something that opened the secret door," said Dick. "And when it opened, the picture had to fall, of course. Golly, it did make me jump!"

A deep sound suddenly boomed through the house. "The gong—it's dinner-time!" said Lucy, with a groan. "Just as we have found this exciting secret door!"

"Better shut it up again," said Dick. "We won't say a word to Aunt Hannah about it till we've explored a bit. We might find family treasure, or something. You never know!"

Visions of glittering jewels, bags of silver and gold, boxes of coins, flashed into the minds of the children. It was very hard to pull at the knob inside the hole and see the secret door shut itself, when they so badly wanted to go through it. They couldn't lift the heavy picture up again, so they left it standing against the wall. Then they went to wash their hands.

Aunt Hannah beamed at them as they took their places at the table.

"Well," she said, "it has stopped raining at last—and I have arranged a treat for you this afternoon."

The children looked blank. A treat? The only treat they wanted was to go through that secret door! Why had the rain stopped? They didn't want to leave the house now.

"I've telephoned to Farthington—that's our nearest big town, you know," said Aunt Hannah, "and I've got tickets for the circus there, for you. A car is coming at half-past two, and you shall have a late tea at a very nice shop in Farthington that has chocolate éclairs and meringues."

Now, ordinarily this would have been a simply glorious treat, but not to-day! Still, since everything was all arranged, the children could only say thank you, and go!

"We'll have to explore this evening," said Dick gloomily. "I can hardly wait! What a pity the circus couldn't have been to-morrow."

It was a lovely circus, and the tea that followed was glorious. Aunt Hannah came too and seemed to enjoy everything very much.

"Now, when we get home, we will have a quiet game of cards together," she said. "I don't want you to get over-excited to-night, after such an exciting afternoon."

So once again exploring had to be put off, and the children played Happy Families and Snap till bed-time. It was terribly disappointing.

Just as Lucy was about to fall asleep in her bed that night, the two boys came cautiously into her room. "Lucy! Are you awake? We're going to go through that secret door now, to-night! We simply can't wait. Do you want to come, or will you be frightened, because it's night?"

"Of *course* I want to come!" said Lucy, wide awake immediately. "I'll put on my dressing-gown at once. Oh, how super! I never, never thought you'd go to-night!"

Trembling with excitement, Lucy followed the two boys downstairs and along the passages that led to the saddle-room. Dick pulled at the nail that opened the secret panel. It swung aside as before. He put in his hand and pulled at the knob behind. With a grating noise the secret door opened in the panelling nearby, and the children stared into the gaping hole.

Dick shone his torch there. "A short passage, then

steps," he said, in excitement. "Come on!"

He climbed through the secret door, and the others followed. The passage was very short, and ended at some narrow, very steep stone steps that led downwards. Dick felt hot with excitement. Where did they lead to!

He went down cautiously, afraid of falling. The others followed. There were fifteen of these steps, then they ended, and another passage came in sight.

"We must be below ground now!" said Dick. "Here's another passage leading away from the house. I do wonder what it used to be for?"

"Oh, most old houses had secret passages or hiding-places," said Robin. "People in olden days often needed to hide their treasures from enemies—or even to hide themselves. Golly, isn't it dark—and the roof's so low just here that I have to bend my head."

It was very weird, walking along the narrow, musty passage so far underground. It curved about to avoid rocky parts. Then suddenly Dick came to a standstill.

"Blow! There's been a fall here! Look. The roof has fallen in and we can't get by."

The others crowded up to him and looked over his shoulder. "Yes we *can* get by," said Robin. "We can kick away the rubble at this side, look, and make a way through. It's easy."

They did manage to make their way through and then, covered with dust, they came to a small underground room! An old bench stood at one side, and a crock for water. On a rough shelf was a dust-covered top and a queer curved stick.

The children gazed at them in delight.

"The top and the stick—which that boy of long ago hid from brother William," said Dick, at last. "How weird. He never came to fetch them again."

They stood in silence, looking round the bare little room—and then Robin gave an amazed cry. He bent down and picked up something. "Look," he said, "do look—a *cigarette end*!"

So it was. The others could hardly believe their eyes. "How did it get here? Who has been here? And when?"

As they stood there they suddenly heard a noise. It seemed to come from above their heads. They looked up and saw that the roof seemed to have a hole in it.

And then, even as they looked, the end of a rope appeared, and the rope itself slid through the hole touching Dick on the shoulder. He shut off his torch at once.

"Someone's coming! But what are they doing here? It's almost midnight. They must be up to something queer!"

"Get back to where that heap of rubble is," whispered Robin. "We can squeeze through again and stay at the other side and listen. Quick!"

With beating hearts the three hurried to the mass of rubble, squeezed through as quietly as they could, and then stood waiting in the dark, listening and peering through the cracks in the heap of rubble that stretched from floor to roof.

Someone slid down the rope. Then a torch flashed on. "Come on, Bill," said a voice. "Buck up with the stuff!"

The man took a candle from his pocket, and set it on the wooden bench. He lighted it, and the children saw by its flickering flame that the man in the underground room was thick-set and very short. As he stood there, waiting, something fell through the hole in the roof, and the man caught it deftly. Then another package came, looking like a sack of something, and then another.

A muffled voice sounded down the hole. "That's all, Shorty. Come on up. We'll fetch it to-morrow."

Shorty hauled himself up the rope, after blowing out the candle. Then there was silence. The children waited for a while, then cautiously made their way back to the underground room again. There were now three sacks there, tied up at the necks.

"They're full of something hard," said Dick, feeling them. "Got a knife on you, Robin?"

Nobody had, because they all wore dressing-gowns. Robin managed to untie one of the sacks. It was full of little jewel boxes. Lucy opened one, and gasped.

Inside was a most beautiful necklace, that glittered brilliantly in the light of the torch. All the other boxes contained jewellery too.

"Looks like the result of a very successful robbery!" said Dick. "What a wonderful place to hide it! I suppose the burglars didn't know there was another way to this room besides that hole in the roof. What shall we do? Drag the sacks back to the house?"

"Oh *yes*," said Lucy. "They will be such a surprise for Aunt Hannah. I'd love to see her face when she sees all these. And it would be too awful to leave them here, in case those men came back and got them!"

So, puffing and panting, the children dragged a sack each through the rubble and up the passage to the stone steps. Up the steps they went, and along to the secret door. They dumped the sacks in the saddle-room, and sat down, panting and excited.

"You go and wake Aunt Hannah, Lucy," said Dick. So she went up to her great-aunt's room and knocked on the door.

"What is it?" came Aunt Hannah's startled voice. "Oh, you, Lucy. Is somebody ill?"

"No. But, Aunt Hannah, do put on your dressing-gown and come down to the saddle-room," begged Lucy.

"To the *saddle*-room—in the middle of the night!" said Aunt Hannah, beginning to think it was all a dream. "Dear, dear—whatever's happening!"

Soon she was down in the saddle-room, astonished to see the sacks there, and even more astonished to see the secret door.

"Good gracious!" she said. "So you've found that! The door has not been used for ages—and has been forgotten so long that nobody ever knew where it was—except you children, apparently! Well, well, well—now tell me what's been happening."

So they told her—and when they showed her what was in the sacks Aunt Hannah could hardly believe her eyes. She gasped and blinked, and couldn't find a word to say.

"I suppose we'd better ring up the police, hadn't we?" said Dick. "We could hand these to them and tell them about the burglar's plan to go to the underground room to-morrow night—and they could catch them beautifully!"

The police were amazed, and very pleased. "Ho—so it was Shorty and Bill, was it?" said the Inspector. "Well, we've been wanting them for a very long time! The stolen goods all belong to the Duchess of Medlington—my word, she'll be glad to have them back! Smart work, children!"

"Well, it was all because of William's brother, really," said Lucy, and the Inspector stared at her in surprise. William's brother? Whatever was the child talking about?

"Now you really must go to bed, children," said Aunt Hannah. "It's two o'clock in the morning. Shocking! No more finding of secret doors and underground rooms and stolen goods to-night, please. Off to bed with you!"

"Well," said Dick, as they got into bed at last, "we thought this would be the dullest place in the world to stay at—but it's given us a most exciting adventure."

So it had—and it was even more exciting when the

Inspector telephoned the next night to say that he had got Bill and Shorty all right. "You can't think how astonished they were when they found that their sacks had vanished out of that hole!" chuckled the Inspector. "And they were even more amazed when my men popped down on top of them."

"Wish I'd been there," said Dick. "I say, Aunt Hannah—do you think I might have that long-ago boy's top? It still spins beautifully."

"Of course," said Aunt Hannah. "And Dick can have the walking-stick, cut so many years ago from the hedge. And as for Lucy, she can have this tiny brooch which has been sent to her by the Duchess herself! There you are, Lucy—now you will none of you ever forget the adventure of the secret room!"

The Twins Get in a Fix

THE TWINS were a pair of pickles. They were staying at the seaside, and what a mischievous pair they were! They knocked down other children's sand castles, and took their pails and hid them. They borrowed their shrimping-nets without asking, and they really made the other children very angry.

"Leave our things alone!" they said. "You are most annoying children and we won't play with you if you behave like this."

But the twins took no notice. They always did what they liked.

Now one afternoon the bigger children decided to make an enormous sand castle, the biggest anyone had ever built on the beach. The twins were asked if they would like to help, for such a big castle needed every-one to dig it. But that was too much like hard work for the twins! "No, thank you," said Jim. "We are going shrimping."

"We think sand castles are babyish," said Joan. So they went off by themselves—but they couldn't help watching that sand castle growing!

It really *was* an enormous one! It was the kind that uncles and aunts and fathers and mothers build when they all get together and borrow our spades. Kenneth and Ronnie, Harry and Jack, Lily and Mary, Doris and Freda, all helped to dig it. The castle grew and grew, and the moat around it became wider and wider and deeper and deeper.

"Gracious!" said Kenneth, stopping for a rest. "I really shouldn't think such a big castle has ever been built before! We shall need steps to get up to the top!"

So they cut steps to go up to the top of it. It looked very grand indeed. The children were sorry when tea-time came and they had to go.

"We'll all come back as soon after tea as we can," said Doris. "Then we can take turns at sitting on the top when the tide comes in."

So they hurried home and left the big sand castle. But, you know, as soon as they had gone those twins ran up to look at it—and they walked up the steps right to the very top!

"Oooh! Isn't it a lovely castle!" said Jim. "Let's call it ours. Let's sit on the top."

"Yes, let's," said Joan. "The tide's coming in, and it will be fun to see it filling the moat and swishing all round the castle."

So the twins sat on the top and watched the waves creeping nearer and nearer. How they screamed with joy when one ran into the moat and lapped all round the castle!

Just then the other children came back, and they shouted with rage when they saw Jim and Joan on the top of their beautiful castle.

"Get down! It's ours!" they cried. "You wouldn't help to build it and you shan't share it!"

"Well, we just *shan't* get down!" said Joan, and she laughed. "And if you try and pull us down we shall kick and knock the castle all to bits. So there!"

"You horrid, nasty children!" said Kenneth. "You know quite well that *we* built this castle, and *we* wanted to sit on the top when the tide came in. Get down at once!"

"Shan't! Shan't! Shan't!" sang the twins, and they made rude faces at the others. The children round the castle were very angry, but they couldn't do anything. They were so afraid that Jim and Joan would spoil their lovely castle if they tried to pull them down.

The waves came higher and higher, and the watching children had to run back up the beach. The tide was getting high. They went back and watched their castle.

"We're the kings of the castle, we're the kings of the

castle!" sang the twins, and they waved their hands cheekily.

Now that evening the tide was really very high. Big waves swept up to the enormous castle, and lapped all round it every time. Soon the sea was surrounding it, and the waves galloped beyond the castle and up the beach. The castle seemed quite a long way out in the sea.

The twins suddenly looked behind them—and, good gracious, the shore seemed simply miles away! The other children were playing a game of catch-ball and were no longer watching them. It really seemed as if Jim and Joan were far away, alone on a crumbling island in the middle of the big sea.

"Oh!" squealed Joan suddenly, very frightened. "The sea's all round! It's deep, it's deep!"

"The castle is breaking to bits—we'll be in the water!" shouted Jim.

"We'll be drowned, because we can't swim!" yelled Joan. "Help!"

The other children heard the twins shouting, and they looked towards the castle. "It's breaking up and the twins will fall into the deep sea," said Kenneth.

"A jolly good thing!" said Doris. "Let them have a fright!"

"Well, we can't let them drown," said Kenneth. "Where's our boat?"

It was pulled high up on the beach. Kenneth and Jack dragged it down to the water and got into it. They rowed out to the twins, who were now half in the water, standing on what was left of the castle. A big wave came and splashed right over them from top to toe. They nearly fell over. Kenneth reached them just in time.

"This jolly well serves you right!" he said as he dragged them into the boat. "Now, before we take you back to the shore, do you promise to leave our things alone in future—or do you want to be dropped in the sea again?"

"We promise!" sobbed the twins. So Kenneth and Jack rowed them to the beach, and they ran home to change their clothes, cold and hungry.

And did they keep their promise? Yes, they did, because, naughty as they were, they knew that to break a promise is a dreadful thing to do. So now they are much nicer, but they will never sit on top of any sand castle they build. I'm not surprised—are you?

Adventure Up a Tree

"HERE's a fine tree to climb," said Alan to Jack. "Let's try this one. I should think it would rock in the wind like a ship."

"Yes—and it doesn't look *too* difficult to get up." said Jack. "It's jolly high, Alan. We should be able to see a long way from the top."

"Come on, then," said Alan. "I'll go first. I'm better than you at climbing. You follow the way I go."

So up he went. The tree was an oak—wide-spread and very leafy. It wasn't really very difficult to climb. Jack followed, and soon the two boys had found a nice broad branch, not far from the top of the tree, where they could sit and eat the sandwiches they had brought.

The wind was strong. It shook the tree, and the boys liked that. "Just like a ship swaying on the sea," said Alan. "I almost expect to hear the splash of the waves!"

The two boys were friends. They loved to go out together and find a hidey-hole of some kind. Today, it was a tree. They liked to take their tea, some chocolate and a book, and have a good read together.

"I've got a new adventure book," said Alan. "I'm in the middle of it. I'll lend it to you afterwards, Jack—it's really exciting!"

"I like adventure stories, too," said Jack. "But I think I'd rather *have* an adventure than read about one. I've never had an adventure in my life . . . I don't believe many people do—do you, Alan?"

"Oh, *yes*," said Alan. "And I'm sure adventures happen suddenly. Why, one might happen to us at *any* moment!"

"Pooh," said Jack, staring down from the tree at the quiet countryside around. "Whatever do you think could happen to us up here, this quiet afternoon? Nothing at all!"

"I can't really think of anything," said Alan. "But adventures *do* seem to happen out of nothing—at least, they do in books."

"Is that a bird whistling?" said Jack, lifting his head to listen. "I've never heard *that* song before!"

It was a flute-like whistle, rather like a blackbird's, and it sounded not very far off. Both boys listened, forgetting their talk about adventures. The whistling stopped, and then began again for a bit.

"I don't believe it's a bird," said Jack. "I think it's someone down in the wood." As he spoke, the boys could hear twigs cracking and the rustling of leaves as somebody pushed his way through the wood below.

"Ssh!" said Alan. "Whoever it is is coming this way. We don't want them to see us. This is our secret hidey-hole today."

The whistling sounded again, exactly the same. "Sounds like a kind of signal to someone," said Jack. "Somebody meeting someone, I suppose."

"Be quiet—he's coming under our tree," whispered Alan. Both boys sat as still as mice. Alan was right—the newcomer was now directly under their tree. Then all at once another whistle sounded. Someone else was coming, too.

"Can you see who they are?" asked Jack, in a whisper. "Are they boys? Do you know them?"

Alan peered down through the branches. All he could see was the top of two heads, and each head wore a cloth cap. Then the boys heard men's voices.

"Where's Jim? He's always late! We'll wait for a few minutes, then leave a note for him."

"Right. He'll have to know what to do, and we've got no way of getting in touch except this meeting-place. What's kept him?"

There was the sound of a match striking and then the smell of cigarette smoke. The men were evidently smoking whilst they waited.

The boys whispered together. "We won't make a sound! The men might be angry if they knew we were over their heads."

"All right. Don't drop your book on them, or you'll give us away. It's slipping off the branch!"

Jack caught his book before it fell. The men below smoked on without a word. After ten minutes or so they got up. "I'll scribble a note," said one, and there was the sound of rustling paper. Then there was a silence. One of them was writing.

After that the two men went, and the boys heard their voices in the distance. They looked at one another. "It seems a bit queer, somehow," said Jack. "What shall we do? Go down and find the note?"

"Well—the third man might come and catch us," said Alan. "One of us would have to stay up the tree and look out for him, I think."

"You go down, then," said Jack. "I'll stay up here. I'll whistle if I see or hear him. Buck up."

Alan shinned quickly down the tree. He wondered if he ought to read somebody else's note—but there really was something a bit peculiar about all this. The two men hadn't sounded nice men—and why should they have a meeting-place in the wood when they ought to be working?

Alan came to the foot of the tree. He looked about for the note, but there was no sign of one. That meant the men must have hidden it somewhere—in some place where the third man would know where to look for it. Alan began to hunt about.

He lifted up a big stone. Nothing there. He parted the leaves of a bush and looked in the middle. Nothing there, either. He saw a rabbit-hole nearby and put his hand down. No—nothing to be found.

"How are you getting on?" called Jack. "Found it?"

"No," said Alan. "I've looked everywhere. I'll just look round the tree-trunk—there might be a cranny somewhere."

He was right. There was a crack in the trunk just wide enough for him to put in his hand. He slipped it in and immediately felt paper. He drew it out. It was a single sheet torn from a notebook. Alan read what was on it.

"Bring car to l.c. gates, 3.10 sharp."

That was all there was. What in the world did it mean? What were l.c. gates? And did 3.10 mean afternoon or early morning? Alan didn't know.

A low whistle disturbed him. "Alan! Someone's coming!" came Jack's guarded voice. Alan thrust the paper back into the trunk of the oak and scrambled up the tree again. The two boys waited in silence for the newcomer.

He came straight to the tree. It must be Jim, then, whoever Jim was—the one the other two had waited for. There was the rustle of paper. Jim had known the hiding-place for it and had drawn it out. There was a moment's silence. Perhaps he was now reading the message. Then there was the rustle of paper again.

After that there was only the sound of footsteps going away and twigs crackling on the ground now and then.

The boys slid down the tree. Jack asked Alan where he had seen the hidden paper, and put his hand into the crack to feel it. At once he felt paper, and drew out the same little sheet that Alan had seen.

But now a few more words had been added. "O.K. Have arranged for us to go to Big Harry's after."

"I don't like this," said Alan. "I shan't put this note back. I shall keep it. It's odd. I'll ask my father about it tonight."

But he couldn't, because his father came home too late that night, and Alan was in bed and fast asleep. Jack was awake, wondering if by *any* chance they had nearly had an adventure that afternoon. It had all ended rather tamely, for both boys had had to hurry back because they were late, and had raced through the wood and through the town to their homes.

In the morning Alan's father read the newspaper as usual. He gave an exclamation. "Well—what will happen next? Somebody set the level-crossing gates against the 3.10 train very early this morning—and when it stopped a couple of men got into the guard's van, knocked him over the head, took a mailbag and escaped. No sign of them at all!"

Alan listened, open-mouthed. The 3.10! Why, 3.10 was in that note surely? Did it refer to the train that went over the crossing in the middle of the night?

"'L.c. gates'—level-crossing gates, of course!" thought Alan. "We might have guessed. I must tell Daddy."

"Daddy," he began, but his father was looking at the clock. "Good gracious, I'm late! I shall miss my train. Goodbye, all of you!"

Alan decided to tell Jack before he said anything. It was Saturday, so he was free. He did the errands for his mother and then shot off to Jack's. He found Jack in a most excited state, for he, too, had seen the papers.

"I say, Alan, that note! That was the plan made for that robbery!" began Jack, as soon as he saw Alan. "I've worked it all out. They shut the gates, stopped the train, and two of them knocked out the guard and robbed the van. The third man—the one the others called Jim—brought the car to the gates, so that he might take the bag and the other two men away—to Big Harry's, wherever that might be."

"Yes, I know!" said Alan, just as excited. "Golly—we were in the middle of an adventure and didn't know it. We'll have to go to the police now, Jack. Thank goodness I've got that note, so they'll believe us."

The police were surprised to see the two boys walking into the police station. "Well, boys, what do you want?" said the constable there.

"We've got something to tell you about the men who robbed the train—the 3.10 last night," said Alan.

"Tell away," said the policeman, getting out his notebook.

"There were three of them," said Alan, "and one is called Jim. They had a car waiting at the gates, and they have all gone to Big Harry's."

The policeman put down his notebook and stared in amazement at Alan. "How do you know all this?"

"We were up a tree near where they met yesterday," said Alan. "They didn't know we were there. They left a note in the tree and we took it. We thought it was all very odd. I meant to tell my father but I fell asleep before he came home. Here's the note."

The policeman whistled in surprise. He took the note and read it. He called through a door. "Hey, come here. There are two boys who know a lot more about last night's happenings than we do!"

Soon Alan was telling his tale from beginning to end. The policeman listened. "Go out to the tree with one of these boys and see what you can find," the chief said to one man. "Cigarette ends, perhaps—or footprints."

"There *are* cigarette ends—and a match, too—and footprints, but not very distinct!" said Jack, wishing he had been sensible enough to pick up the cigarette ends and match for himself. They were clues, of course!

"Could you boys recognise these fellows if you saw them again?" asked the chief.

They shook their heads. "No," said Alan. "We only saw the tops of their heads, you see—we were up the tree. But we saw their caps, of course. They all wore cloth caps."

"Would you know those again?" asked the chief at once.

"Oh, yes," said Alan. "We stared down at them for quite a long time! One had a navy blue cap with a tear in it."

"And one had a tweed cap, awfully dirty," said Jack. "And the third one had a brown cap, rather new, with a big button on the top—brown and flat."

"I want you to stay here for a few minutes," the chief said to Alan. "The other boy can go to the oak tree with this constable and bring back anything they find. Then we will all hop over to Big Harry's. So Big Harry knows about this, does he? Well, well—I often wondered what went on at Big Harry's!"

"What *is* Big Harry's?" asked Jack.

"Just a place where men can sleep for the night," said the chief. "It's a pity you wouldn't recognise these three again—but if you can spot their caps that will be just as good."

Jack and the policeman went to the tree and collected two cigarette ends and a match. "They smoke Coastguard cigarettes, sir," reported the constable, when they got back to the station. "And this is a special kind of match, sir—rather big."

"Right," said the chief. "Good. Now, you two boys, I want you to come with me and do a little cap-spotting. Ready?"

Well, it was a real thrill to go in the big black police car and roar down the road to the next town. Alan and Jack looked at one another in delight. Whoever would have thought such a thing would happen?

They came to a narrow, rather dirty street. At one end was a tall, ugly building. This was Big Harry's.

The police pushed their way into a dark, dirty hall. Pegs ran all the way down, hung with dirty coats and caps and hats. The chief shone a torch onto them. "Spot the caps, boys," he said. "That one," said Jack, pointing to a tweed one. "And that one! That's the brown one with the flat button."

"And here's the navy one," said Alan. "There you are, sir, those are the ones."

"Thanks," said the chief. "Now we'll just find Big Harry and tell him to turn out all his boarders into the street. He won't know why and we shan't tell him! All we want to see is who takes those three caps. Then we shall know what to do!"

To the two boy's enormous disappointment, they

had to go back and wait in the police car. They didn't see Big Harry, frightened and blustering when the police told him to turn out all the men who had slept there the night before. Some were still in bed! However, they were all turned out, and, grumbling and grousing, they went to fetch their coats and caps and hats.

Of course, the three thieves took their own caps—and what a shock for them when the police arrested them and charged them with the robbery of the night before! One of them was smoking a Coastguard cigarette, and another had a box of matches on him full of matches exactly like the one found under the tree.

"Well, boys," said the chief, when the two boys were back at the police station, excited and thrilled. "You did well to spot those caps! Made our job very, very easy! Those young men will not be wearing caps for a very long time. And a good thing, too."

The boys said goodbye and left together. "What will our parents say?" said Jack. "How do you like adventures, Alan? We were in the middle of one yesterday without knowing it!"

"I like them very much—so long as I'm on the right side," said Alan. "I would rather catch a thief than be one. What cowards they were to attack the guard of the train like that! My word, Jack—let's have another adventure, shall we?"

"We'll look out for one," said Jack. And they are looking very hard. I do hope they find another soon, don't you?

The Astonishing Guy

ELLEN, Harry, Jack, Leslie, George, and Fanny were getting excited about Guy Fawkes' Day. They were saving up their money to buy as many fireworks as possible. What fun to set them all off in the garden on Bonfire Night!

"We can get a lot of different kinds, you know," said Harry. "There are sparklers, and golden rain, and catherine wheels, and rockets, and——"

"Ooooh! It sounds fine," said Ellen. "Let's see how much money we've got already."

So they counted it up, and found that they had almost two shillings. "That will buy quite a lot," said Ellen. "There is a box of fireworks for half a crown that looks lovely—perhaps we can save a few pennies more and buy that."

"I think we ought to have a guy, too," said Jack. "We'll have a real beauty and we'll make every bit of him ourselves. We can easily do that."

"Oh yes," said Fanny. "That would be fun."

So they began to make a guy. He really was a funny one! They stuffed his body with straw, and made him a round head on which they put a funny mask. Daddy gave Ellen an old hat, and Mummy gave George a pair of old trousers for the guy.

Harry's uncle gave the children a worn-out coat and a torn shirt, and the children found two old boots in a ditch, which they pushed on to the guy's legs.

When he was finished he looked very real. He sat in the wood-shed, grinning at them, and, as Ellen said, he looked almost as if he was going to get up and join them in their play.

He sat on an old broken chair, waiting for Guy Fawkes' Day. The children saved up more money, and then found that they had three shillings and a penny!

"I'll go and buy our fireworks this afternoon," said Harry, pleased. So off he went, with Ellen; but do you know, there was a big hole in Harry's pocket—and by the time he got to the shop there was only the penny left there!

Harry put his hand deep into his pocket in dismay. "I say! The money's gone!" he cried. "Oh, Ellen—there's a hole in my pocket! There's only a penny left. All the rest is gone!"

"It must have fallen out when we were running across the field," said Ellen anxiously. "I thought I heard a clinking noise then. Let's go back and look."

But although they looked for a whole hour, not one bit of the lost money could they find—which was not at all surprising because most of it had rolled down a rat-hole. The children were very unhappy. They went back to tell the others.

"Oh, Harry! You might at least have put the money into a *safe* pocket!" cried George.

"Well, I didn't know this one had a hole in it," said poor Harry. "It must have come quite suddenly."

The children looked at one another sadly.

"Well, we can't buy many fireworks with a penny," said Fanny. "But at least we have still got the guy."

They went to look at him. He sat there on his chair, grinning away at them. He looked a very good-tempered fellow. Harry looked round the shed—and then he noticed something funny.

"I say! Where are Daddy's tools?" he said. "They don't seem to be here."

The children looked round for their father's tools. The spade, the fork, the hoe, and the rake had disappeared. It was very funny. They ran off to tell their mother—and George, Fanny, and Leslie ran next door, where they lived, to see if the tools in *their* shed were all right.

And the funny thing was that some of the tools had been taken from there too. Every one got very excited, and began to talk about robbers and thieves at once.

"We shall have to tell the police," said the children's mothers.

"I do wish we could catch the thief," said Harry. "Daddy is so busy digging his garden in the week-ends now, and I'm sure he won't want to spend money to buy new tools."

Then George had a good idea. "Harry," he said, "maybe the thief will come again to-night to steal a few more things. What about keeping a watch for him?"

"Oh yes," said Harry. "I'll hide in the shed! I'll hide behind the old guy. You come too, George, because it's your idea. And if the robber comes, we'll pretend we are the guy, and make him talk in a big deep voice to frighten him!"

The children giggled. They thought this was a marvellous idea! So that night George and Harry crept down to the shed, dressed in warm clothes, and went to hide themselves behind the guy.

"Now, if anyone comes, I'll pretend to be the guy talking," said Harry, with a giggle. "That will give the thief such a fright. George, have you brought your big whistle with you? You have? Good. Well, when I nudge you hard—like this—you must blow your whistle, and then the girls will tell our mothers and fathers that the robber is in the shed."

The boys settled down comfortably on some sacks behind the guy. They waited and waited. It was dark, not very warm, and not at all comfortable. They wondered if the thief would come. There were still some tools left to take, so perhaps he would creep along to steal them.

"What a long time to wait!" whispered Harry to George. "I've got pins and needles in my foot."

"I've got pins and needles all over!" said George, with a groan. "In fact, I feel just like a pin-cushion feels! I'm just——"

"Sh!" said Harry suddenly. He had heard a sound. The boys waited silently. The sound came again. It was someone coming quietly down the path to the shed, his feet making a tiny noise on the path as he came.

"It's the thief!" whispered Harry.

Then the door was opened gently, with a little creak. Someone came into the shed and shut the door quietly behind him. He switched on a torch, and the beam shone on the guy sitting in his chair at the end of the shed.

"Hallo, guy! So you're still here?" said the voice of the robber. "Well, good evening to you!"

Harry pretended to be the guy.

"Good evening," said the guy in a deep, hoarse voice.

The thief nearly dropped his torch. He stared at the guy in amazement and fright.

"I thought you spoke," he said. "My ears are playing me tricks."

"Ha, ha, ha!" laughed the guy, making a deep sort of noise down his throat. "I *did* speak! Why shouldn't I speak?"

"Oh dear! I don't like this!" said the thief nervously. "It's horrible!"

"No—*you're* horrible!" said the guy. "Coming here like this, and stealing people's tools. Gr-r-r-r!"

The guy growled like a dog, and the thief felt more frightened than ever. George thought Harry was doing marvellously.

The thief quickly took down a pair of good shears from the side of the shed. He meant to steal them, whatever the guy said.

"Put those back!" said the guy in a deep, angry voice.

"Talk all you like—you can't stop me taking things!" said the thief.

"What! Can't I?" roared the guy, and he stood up! Yes—he really did! It was Harry pushing him up, of course, but the thief didn't know that. He really thought the guy was standing up himself. He gave a scream.

"Stop! Don't come any nearer! I'll put the shears back."

Harry made the guy wobble a bit as if he was going to walk forward. The thief quickly put back the shears. The guy had an old stick in his hand. Harry lifted the guy's arm with the stick in it, making it seem as if he was going to hit the thief.

The man was so frightened that he couldn't find the

door. He began to groan with fright and to feel all round for the door. And then Harry gave George a sharp nudge—that meant he was to blow his whistle.

"Stay where you are," said the guy, in an angry voice. "I am going to whistle for help. If you so much as move out of this shed, I will come after you and beat you with my stick."

George blew a shrill blast on his big whistle. The guy waved his stick about—though it was really Harry waggling it. The thief didn't know what to do— he was afraid of turning round to open the door in case the guy came after him, and he was afraid too, that the whistle would bring someone else! So he stayed where he was, trembling with fright.

The girls rushed to tell their parents that they had heard the whistle. Two big fathers at once went down the garden, astonished but fierce—and flung open the shed door. There was the thief, cowering against a pile of baskets!

"Oh—so it's you, Brown!" said Harry's father, and he caught hold of the man's shoulders. "I gave you notice because I knew you were stealing vegetables from the garden—so you thought you'd come back and steal a few more things! Well—the police will deal with you!"

"I say!" said George's father in astonishment. "Look at that guy! It's alive!"

"Yes, sir—it's almost frightened me out of my skin!" said the thief in a trembling voice. "It talks—and it came after me with a stick—and it whistled for help. I'm right scared of it."

"You're a wicked man!" said the guy in a deep voice, and he shook his stick again. His hat fell over one eye, and he looked most peculiar. Harry's father knew Harry's voice—and he guessed at once the trick that the boy had played. He grinned to himself, but said nothing to the thief. Let him think that it was the guy who had found him out!

The thief was marched off. The boys came out laughing, and George rushed to tell the others all that Harry had done.

The children's fathers laughed over the astonishing guy. "For a moment he gave me a shock," said George's father. "I really thought he had come alive! No wonder the thief was scared."

"Well, you boys did a good job of work to-night," said Harry's father, pleased. "I hope you will enjoy your fireworks and your guy on November the Fifth."

"We shall enjoy the guy—but we shan't have

fireworks," said Ellen sadly. "We saved three shillings and a penny—and lost all the money except the penny."

"Well, that's too bad," said her father. "Look—here is half a crown, Harry, for your smart work to-night. Buy some fireworks with it."

"And, George, here is half a crown for *you*," said George's father. "You deserve a reward as well."

"Goodness! Five whole shillings!" squealed the children. "What luck!"

"More than we had before!" said Fanny.

"We'll spend it to-morrow," said Leslie.

"But we won't let Harry put it into his pocket," said Ellen, bringing out a purse for the money. "We mustn't lose it again."

And now they're off to-day to spend the five shillings. Aren't they lucky? They *will* get a fine lot of fireworks—and wouldn't I just love to see them!

The Train that Broke in Half

BENNY was a funny little boy. He thought he couldn't do anything well! He was always afraid of things, so he was shy and timid, and hadn't any friends.

"Benny, why don't *you* go in for the races?" his mother said each summer when the school sports came. But Benny shook his head.

"No, I'm no good at running," he said. "I'd only be last, and look silly, Mother."

"Benny, why don't you ask to belong to the Scout Cubs?" said his father when the spring came and the Scouts and Cubs put on their uniforms and went to have some fun in the fields.

"I'd be no good," said Benny. "I'd never learn enough. You have to know a lot."

"Well, you could learn, as the others do," said his father. But no—Benny wouldn't try. He was afraid of looking silly and of being laughed at.

It was the same with everything. When he went to parties, Benny wouldn't play Musical Chairs because he felt sure he would be the first one out. At Christmastime he wouldn't pull a cracker because he didn't like the bang.

"But, Benny, you've never pulled a cracker in your life, so how do you know you won't like the bang?" asked his mother. "You may love it, as the other children do. Don't be such a little coward."

Well, that was quite the wrong thing to say to shy Benny. He at once thought he *was* a little coward, so he became more ashamed and shy than ever. He thought that everyone must think him a coward, so he wouldn't play games in case he fell down and cried, and he wouldn't go to any parties at all.

It was dreadful. His mother didn't know what to do with such a funny boy. The other children got tired of asking him to play with them and left him quite alone. So Benny played by himself all day long, and hardly opened his mouth at school. And yet, secretly, Benny longed to have friends and to shout and run and play. Poor Benny!

Now, not far from Benny's house ran a railway line, deep down in a cutting. Benny loved to watch the trains that ran by. He liked to hear their shrill whistling, and to see the smoke come curling up. He knew every one of the trains, and would have liked to wave to the engine-driver, but he was much too shy.

One day he was sitting on the fence, watching the trains, when the long train from the nearest big city came by. It was a corridor train, so that the carriages were closely joined together for people to walk all up and down the train if they wanted to. Benny liked that sort of train, because he could see the people sitting at the dining-tables and having their dinner, and he could see people standing in the corridors and looking out of the window.

With a loud whistle the train came along, deep down in the cutting. Benny looked at his watch. The train was late, and it was hurrying. Not more than ten minutes behind it would come the next train.

"You'd better hurry!" said Benny to the train. He wouldn't talk to other children, but he often talked to animals and trains and cars. The train whistled and went on.

And then a strange thing happened. The three last carriages of the train suddenly broke away and got left behind!

Benny stared as if he couldn't believe his eyes! The rest of the train went rushing on, and was soon out of sight. Just those three carriages were left behind. They ran a little way, and then stopped on the line.

"It's broken in half," said Benny to himself. "The

train's broken in half! Where's the guard? Will he pop his head out of the guard's van and see what's happened?"

But no guard popped his head out. He couldn't because he was in the other part of the train. He had gone to speak to the ticket-collector who happened to be on the train—so he didn't know anything about his van being left behind.

Nobody was in the last three carriages at all. They were quite empty. There they stood on the line, looking rather silly.

Benny soon saw that there was nobody in them. He stared and stared—and then had a dreadful thought.

What about the next train that would come rushing along in a few minutes' time? It wouldn't know those carriages were left on the line. Nobody knew but Benny. The signal-man didn't know. The engine-driver wouldn't know—and he would go crashing into them!

"Then there would be an accident," said Benny. "Oh dear! Whatever shall I do?"

For once Benny forgot that he thought himself a poor little coward, no good at anything. He only thought of the people in the train that was soon coming into that deep railway cutting, and would crash into the carriages there. Benny sprang down from the fence. "If I run for all I'm worth I could perhaps get to the signal-box in time, and tell the man to put the signal up against the next train!" thought the little boy. "That would stop it!"

He began to run. Benny hadn't thought he was any good at running at all—but how he ran now! His legs twinkled in and out, and his breath came in big pants. His chest felt as if it would burst, but Benny didn't care. No—he must, he must, he *must* get to that signal-box in time!

It was quite a long way—but at last Benny saw it in the distance. His legs were so tired that they could hardly run, but he made them go on and on until he reached the signal-box. The signal-man was leaning out of his box, and he saw Benny.

Now in the ordinary way Benny wouldn't have dared to speak to a signal-man—but now he didn't care what he did. He could hear the train coming!

He turned his head, and there it was, rushing along the line—the train that would crash into the three carriages! Benny tried to shout, but his voice was so full of puffs and pants that he could hardly get his words out.

"Signal-man, put the signal up!" he panted. "Put it up! There's some carriages left on the line—broken off the last train!"

The signal-man could hardly understand the breathless boy, but he at once pulled a heavy lever—and to Benny's great delight the signal that had been down for the train to pass by, went up with a click—just as the train came rumbling up at a great speed.

The driver saw the signal going up and he put on his brakes very suddenly. With a long screech the train slowed down and then stopped. Passengers popped their heads out of the windows to see what was the matter.

Benny got back his breath. He yelled to the signal-man: "The last train broke in half! It left three carriages behind up the line. I only just got here in time to warn you."

"Good for you, young man!" said the signal-man. He ran down from his box and went to the engine-driver. Then the train steamed slowly on, taking the signal-man too, and soon everyone saw the three left-behind carriages.

"That was a narrow escape," said the engine-driver, looking pale. "I'd have been right into those carriages if you hadn't put the signal against me."

"It's that boy who saved the train," said the signal-man, looking round for Benny. But Benny was gone! You won't believe it, but all his shyness and fear came back again when he saw so many passengers looking at him. He ran home quickly and went into his bedroom. He was trembling now. He couldn't think how he could have done such a thing!

That tea-time his mother was full of the whole affair. "Fancy, Benny," she said, "a boy saved the London train! He saw some carriages left behind on the line, and he tore to the signal-man to tell him—and the next train was saved. Oh, Benny—if only you could do a thing like that! How proud Daddy and I would be of you!"

Benny looked at his mother. He knew how often he had disappointed her because he had been so silly and shy and afraid. Now he had a big surprise in store for her!

"Would you really be proud of me?" he said. "I'd like that, Mother!"

"Oh, Benny, I'd be so proud I'd run out and tell everyone about you!" said his mother. "But you're such a funny little quiet boy—you'd never do anything wonderful, you'd be too scared!"

Just then a knock came at the door—and who should be there but the signal-man! He knew Benny and knew where he lived—and he had come to say a few words to him. And behind him was a crowd of children—the boys and girls of Benny's school, who had already heard about Benny from the signal-man!

"Where's Benny?" said the signal-man. "Ah, there you are! You're a hero, Benny! You saved the train! My goodness, I saw you running to my box, and I've never seen anyone run so fast in my life! Never! You'd win any race if you ran like that. I want to shake hands with you."

And he solemnly shook hands with Benny, whilst Benny's mother and father looked on in the greatest surprise.

"But was it our *Benny* who saved the train?" cried the boy's father. "Good gracious! To think Benny could do that! Benny, Benny, I'm proud of you! I always thought you were a timid little fellow—but my word, you're a hero!"

His mother hugged him. His father clapped him on the back. The signal-man shook his hand up and down—and in crowded all the boys and girls, yelling, "Benny, Benny! Tell us all about it. Come out, Benny, we want to see you."

And then, in the twinkling of an eye, Benny became a hero. He didn't feel a cowardly little fellow any more. He wasn't afraid of anything. He wanted to shout and run and climb. He was changed from top to toe!

"I didn't know I could do it—but I did!" he kept telling himself. "I was wrong about myself. I was silly and shy just because I thought myself to be silly and shy—but I'm not really. I'm brave and bold—I can run very fast. I can do fine things! Oh, I'm glad, I'm glad! Everything will be different now!"

And so it is—for Benny himself is different, you see. The passengers of the train collected money to give to the boy who saved them, and they bought Benny a fine toy motor-car that he drives down the streets every day. And to hear him come hooting along at a fine pace, you'd never think he was once a poor, shy little fellow who couldn't say boo to a goose!

You never know what you can do till you try!